The King's Pen Pal

Peter J. Osterlund

To Bella and Anna, the ones that sparked this story.

Other works by Peter J. Osterlund

Broken Planets

Lost Orbit

Bad News and Terrible Ideas

To Karness,

Firstly, I fear I have to apologise for how long it has taken me to write this letter. Every day the words flee from me like a dying breath and I grow more and more frustrated that I cannot simply speak with you as if you were here now.

To answer your question, yes, I am doing well; however, If you were here with me now, you'd probably disagree. In all *honestly I feel that I am growing tired of this phenomenon called life. Don't worry I am not thinking of that, I am merely growing weary of what I am doing with it.*

In truth, I have never been satisfied with my life. I look back at all that's passed and think nothing of it.

So many days wasted. So many times I wish I was elsewhere. So many days I wish I could be standing with you, telling you everything on my mind.

I'm rambling I know, but then again you knew what you were signing up for when we began this journey.

I exhaled as I looked over the fresh ink. Whenever it was time to write one of these, all sense of grammar and literacy skills were thrown out the door. I found myself staring at the words like they were strangers, trying to make sense of what the hell I had just written.

I couldn't tell if it was because every time I received a new letter from Karness, my whole body filled with something close to ecstasy, or if it was simply that my eyes were struggling to stay open. Perhaps I should take my medication now and resume.

Before I could return to one of the few joys of my stretched life, there was a knock at my door—a door I hadn't been able to physically open in years.

"My liege," came a voice I assumed belonged to one of my guards.

"Yes," I managed to say without coughing up a lung. "The doctors are here."

Ahh yes, I thought with no particular excitement. "Bring them in." This time, I coughed—hard enough to paint my hand with a fresh coat of blood.

I was met by two figures, completely covered from head to toe in layers of cloth, even though my illness was considered non-contagious. No one could blame them for the precaution; after all, if anyone saw my condition, their first instinct would be to run, followed closely by the urge to cover up and avoid all contact.

They took my quill and parchment from my lap before placing it on my bedside table. Despite how much I wished to continue writing to Karness, I knew this medical evaluation couldn't be postponed.

"My liege," one of the doctors said, "could you lift your arm for me, please?"

The temptation to say 'I have no bloody idea,' was up there, but that would've been cruel and these doctors had already done so much for me after all these years.

I managed to raise my arm by a full two inches from my side.

"A new personal best?" I asked with a weak smile. The doctors didn't seem to share my sense of humour. Through their masks and thick goggles, it was hard to tell what was considered good or concerning with my condition. But if weekly checkups have taught me anything, it's that silence was never good.

"Say ahh," another doctor said.

I followed his instruction, and by the gods, when I tell you my lungs and pancreas nearly climbed into my throat, the blood and mucus testify that the scene was horrifically disgusting.

I hope these doctors are wearing at least three more layers.

They wiped my mouth and cleaned the mess I'd made before proceeding with the evaluation. By the crown, these sessions felt longer each time—and with them, I felt I had less life left to live.

After more prodding and examining my body, the doctors finally stepped back. They exchanged looks as if waiting for the other to speak.

Gods, how bad is it?

"Go on, Doctor," I said to the one on the left, "How bad is it?"

"My liege...it seems..."

"The infection has spread to over ninety per cent of your body." The other doctor continued. "Everything except your brain has been affected by the illness. But I'm afraid it will continue to spread."

"And when it does?" I asked, already knowing the answer, but hoping the expertise of medical sciences would prove otherwise.

"You will die."

Just as I thought. Perhaps I should've been a doctor.

"How long before that?" I asked.

"Our estimations," the doctors looked to each other, "thirty days."

If I had the strength, my eyes would have shot open. But they didn't. I stood still and swallowed the words like expired medicine.

One month. Last time, I was given years, but now, I only have a month.

"Would you like us to send for your son?"

Perse shouldn't have to see this. He's been prepared for my death for many years now. Grief has already visited him.

"No," I responded, "I require some time to consume this news. Send word to Seris in an hour or so. I wish to speak with him. And only him, do you understand?"

Seris, my sorcerer, needed to be informed of my impending death. He was the one I trusted to prepare the kingdom for its next ruler and the rite of inheritance. And to be honest, I always found a strange comfort in his company. Perhaps, when he arrived, he could offer me some wise words—or better yet, put me out of my misery with a spell.

"As you wish, your grace," the doctors said, bowing before turning to leave my quarters.

"Wait," I coughed, turning toward where my letter lay. "I haven't finished."

One of the doctors approached the bedside table and handed me the letter and quill. They left my quarters, probably for the last time—unless, by some miracle, they discovered a cure for my illness.

I sighed, more lost for words than I usually was with these letters.

But I read what I wrote and felt the news of my mortality wash away from me. Despite never meeting Karness, she always had a way to make me relax and forget this world that I lived in.

Gods, to think how many years it's been since we first wrote to each other. I remember thinking you'd never respond.

But you did. And to this day, I've never regretted one word I've written to you.

"Dammit," I whispered, allowing the thought of time to strike me like a hammer. *Thirty days and I'm writing. I should be enjoying my life. As a person. Not a king. I should...*

For a mere second, my eyes brightened. *Oh. Oh, that could work.*

I began to scratch away at the letter with my quill, allowing the words to conjure themselves from my very fingertips. I smiled. I laughed. If I could, I would have skipped across the room in my underwear.

Luckily, that wasn't the case. A knock came at my door, and so did a gentle voice that I immediately recognised. "My liege?"

"Seris?" I asked, putting the letter underneath my blanket.

"The one and only."

"Come in, please."

A lengthy man entered the room, wearing an outfit of deep blue robes, lined with an almost gold-like fabric. He wore a pair of black-rimmed glasses that were perfectly round. Seris' usual attire always made him appear ready to either study or nap, but given his brilliant mind, it was obvious which possibility was more likely.

"How are you feeling, your grace?" Seris asked with a bland expression.

He already knows. Of course, he does.

"I'm dying. How am I supposed to feel?"

"Well, hopeful for one. The doctors are doing everything in their power to create a cure."

"They've been doing that for the better part of a decade. I doubt a month is going to make any difference."

Seris hummed as if to agree with my point. "I take it you wish to make preparations?"

"Yes," I said between coughs, "but not for Perse."

Seris' head cocked to what looked like an uncomfortable angle. Gods, how could a man with such a slender body, not snap in two?

"I asked you here because you're the only one I can trust with what I'm about to say."

Seris leaned in closer, a little too closely, judging from how quickly he covered his nostrils.

I sighed, "I need you to fake my death."

Retirement

To Keltick,

Even after all this time, the sight of your letters arriving at my door fills me with such joy. Despite your lacklustre efforts to decorate, I cannot help but stare at its majesty.

To answer your letter, yes I have been keeping well, for the most part. A week ago, a terrible storm arrived and damaged most of the town. We lost a couple of farmers who were out at the time, but otherwise, no one else was hurt.

I didn't know any of the farmers who died, but I can't help but imagine how devastated their families must be.

I know it isn't polite to ask, with how close you are to the King, but I know I wouldn't be able to sleep if I didn't.

Would you be able to ask him for assistance? Even if he were to send a mere emissary to my town, I know we would all be grateful. I would be grateful.

Gods, I wish you were here, not because I know you would do nothing else but help us rebuild, but because I need you.

Promise me one day you'll come visit me. Please.

Sometimes, I think you're all I have.

Write to me faster next time mister, or the next storm will be me at the capital.

From Karness.

P.S. Just kidding.

I promise, I thought to myself, trying to imagine what Karness looked like. Was she blonde? Did she have any birthmarks on her face? Was she tall or short? Was she secretly an old man with a hoarding problem? Your guess is as good as mine.

"Excuse me, sire? Seris shook his head. "I don't believe I heard you correctly. Did you say—."

"I need you to fake my death," I repeated.

Seris' eye flickered as if processing my words. "My liege…I don't understand."

I inhaled, before coughing up a great deal of phlegm. Gods, how could a body produce such disgusting substances? It was almost as bad as what came out of my—

"Sire!" Seris called out, regaining my attention.

"Forgive me, Seris. My mind *and* body have succumbed to this illness. I find myself drifting in and out of this world at times."

"It's okay." Seris took off his glasses before polishing them with his robe. "Now, what do you mean by *fake your death?*

"Exactly that," I said with a smile.

The sorcerer stared at me as though he had conjured a spell. An ancient, powerful spell that was called 'What the hell does that mean?'

I sighed, "There's nothing left for me to do here, Seris."

"Yes, there is. There is the preparation of the Kingdom. Your son."

"I have been preparing both for this since I first put on the crown."

Gods, that had been over ten years ago now.

"To them, I'm already dead," I sighed. "I do not wish to spend the last days of my life in bed, regretting choices I did and didn't make."

Seris nodded as though he knew exactly what I was talking about. His eyes scanned what was once the face and body of a king. But now all that was left was a dead man—a dead man who just wanted to live a little before it was too late.

My eyes glanced to one of the open windows of my room, feeling the start of the night's cool air. "I want to leave this place. I want to go out into the country I conquered. Live. Thrive. I want to walk the world as a man, and not a king."

"But my Liege," Seris grabbed one of the bed's posts. "You are in no state to travel. If you were to leave this room, let alone the city, you may die quicker than anticipated."

"How much quicker?" I asked, genuinely curious. It would be good to know if I could end this pain sooner rather than later.

"I don't know. Days, weeks. Depends on how far you wish to travel, and how."

Not far, I thought, *assuming I can find her.*

"I intend to walk," was all I said.

Seris almost laughed at that. Fortunately, he was trained well enough to contain his intrusiveness in front of the King. "I beg your pardon?"

"You heard me," I said abruptly. "I wish to walk. To roam this world one last time."

At that thought, the knowledge of my death came over me like a chilled breeze. To think that I was so close to

the end. How would it happen? Would I start coughing uncontrollably, then suddenly stop breathing? Or
would I collapse to the floor first?

Death was such an odd concept to me. Everyone
made it out to be this horrible ending, whereas I saw it
as simply the end of a journey we were all taking. To me,
death was like tea. Sure, at first, it was this disgusting
cup of hot brown water, but give it time, and you could
come to appreciate it.

Of course, my tea always needed a couple of spoon-
fuls of sugar to make it tolerable.

I suddenly snapped out of my trance, focusing back
on Seris and his comfortable-looking robes.

"Impossible." Seris snapped. "There's no possible
way you can accomplish this, my king. With all due
respect, I can't remember the last time you got out of
bed by yourself."

"How dare you," I grumbled. "I'll have you know I
got out of bed last..." When was that? Last week? New
Year's? The previous New Year's? Gods, all the days
had mixed together like food in my bowels. I scoffed.
"That's just not good enough, Seris," I sighed, staring at
the sorcerer with half-closed eyes. "Please. Let me have
this." A drop of either pus or tears fell down my face.

Judging from my quivering lip, I guessed that it was the latter.

"My liege," Seris whispered, disturbed by what he was witnessing. "I...I can't. Even if I wanted to help, you'd never be able to escape the castle, let alone the city. The only way you'd be able to is..."

I lay there for God knows how long, waiting for Seris to complete his pitiful sentence. "Is?" I stretched the word like a contortionist.

A deep thud came from in front of me, sounding awfully like someone slapping themselves on the forehead. Next, there came Seris saying, "Idiot! Why didn't I think of that before?"

If I had the strength to shrug, I would have.

"Give me a minute, Sire." Seris rushed to the door. "I'll return before the Sun descends. Wait for me."

"I'm not going anywhere," I said, "but wait, what are you—?"

Before I could answer, Seris had left the chamber and shut the door behind him.

Good, I thought. *No one will be able to witness me whimper away.*

I awoke after who knows how long to the sound of the doors opening. There was less of an announcement this time and more of an uncomfortable squeaking you hear when trying to sneak to the latrine.

Not that I did any of that; I'm just using this as an example to set the mood. Actually, forget I said anything.

I was sleeping. The door opened and so I awoke.

Footsteps tapped like droplets along the floor, nearing me as my eyes struggled to adjust.

A blurred image began to form shape in front of me. It stood at the end of my bed, wearing a cloak of pure midnight.

An assassin? I thought, glancing to my side where I'd hidden my knife for so many years. *No.* That wasn't me anymore. I hadn't hidden—let alone held—anything as dangerous as a spork in years.

The person began to move to the bedside, reaching closer and closer to me. I tried to speak out but failed to find my voice—likely because there was an embarrassing amount of mucus stored in my oesophagus.

The assassin laid a hand on my chin gently, caressing it almost. "Shh. Drink this, my liege. Drink all of it."

Seris?

As my vision slowly adjusted to the darkness, I could visualise a bottle in front of me. It was a round-bottom bottle, half-empty with a liquid of pure purple.

The colour was beautiful if not slightly discomforting, with the slight glitter it held and the knowledge that I would have to drink this.

The potion grew closer to my mouth, and I quickly prayed to the Gods that whatever this was, it was at least cherry-flavoured.

It wasn't.

Instead, it tasted of...life. Memories. Energy. Power. Youth. Everything I hadn't felt in years.

What is this? And where can I get the recipe?

I gasped as I met the end of the concoction, shoving Seris and the bottle away with all my strength.

A crash, as well as glass shattering, sounded immediately after.

"Woah!" Seris exclaimed, tumbling backwards before colliding with the floor.

My vision became blurred. I was blinded—no, not blinded. I was...I was. Gods, what was happening to me? My eyes felt like lightning was coursing through every nerve, and yet I felt no pain. It felt as though I'd been sitting my whole life and had just stood up for the first time.

This was, of course, partly true, but that shouldn't distract you from the fact that my body was feeling whole once again.

"Seris?" I called, staring down as he lay on the floor, surrounded by broken glass. "What happened?" Are you okay?"

"Sire..." Seris' eyes were as large as his lenses. "You...you pushed me."

"What?" I cocked my head at him before looking down at my hands.

My body retreated a full inch as I caught sight of my palms, turning them over so I could scan every crevice.

These aren't my hands.

They were as hard as iron and sharper than morning's steel. They could be used for cutting wood all day and leave no signs of blisters. There were no marks, no burns, cuts, festering wounds or rotten nails. Every inch of the hands in front of me was pure and utterly perfect.

And somehow, they were mine. Or at least had become attached to me.

I began to clench my fists, returning to my days as a soldier. The muscles in my hands, along with the arms they were attached to, were firm—ready to grip a blade.

Gods, this felt good.

"Seris," I paused, only now realising how strange my voice felt. No that wasn't a seed stuck in my throat; that was definitely my voice. I grinned at the sorcerer, no longer struggling to do so. "You magnificent bastard. What have you done to me?"

The Plan

What do you look like, Keltick?

I don't know why, but to me, you seem like an educated fellow. I know that doesn't constitute an appearance, but it's a feature I can't ignore.

My guess is you're tall. Not freakish tall, but tall in comparison to the average man. Weight? I wouldn't dare ask. Can you fit through a door?

Just kidding.

Hair? My guess would be that it's short, blonde and has a few curls at its ends. That or you're bald, much like my father.

As for your body, considering how often you and I write, not to mention that you're a scribe for the king. A hunchback? A tall, blonde, educated hunchback?

Wouldn't that be a sight?

Gods, I wish I could see what you look like. And not through some clever trick, like if you were to cover your face with ink and rub it on paper, or have an artist draw you. I want to see you here, in front of me, across this table.

If you were here, perhaps things would be so much easier. For the both of us.

I feel like our lives would be better. And maybe, I don't know, something beautiful could come of it.

And maybe if you have the patience, I could teach you how to decorate your letters.

Now for your turn, mister. What do you think I look like? What does that head of yours imagine when you read these words?

"Sire..." Seris gasped, staring at me with his thick lenses. "You're...you're healthy."

"You sound surprised," I said, shuffling myself towards the edge of the bed.

"No, no, no. I'm just...I didn't think it would *actually* work."

I looked down at the floor, staring at it like a city ready to be conquered. I inhaled, before pushing myself off the bed. My feet echoed against the wooden floorboards, reverberating throughout my body but without any sign of pain.

I gasped. *How long had it been since I could stand?*

I gazed at Seris. My eyes felt so fresh; it was like I'd been asleep my entire life and had finally woken up.

Judging by the way Seris retreated, I must have appeared quite threatening.

"Didn't think *what* would work?" I asked.

"I...I...I...I," Seris repeated, face becoming drained of colour.

"Seris!" I called out with a kingly voice.

His body snapped to attention, rising from the floor with perfect posture. All he needed was a military uniform, and you'd think he was a soldier. Perhaps I should get him to do some pushups, that'll toughen the scrawniness out of him.

"Tell me," I said, far calmer now, "what did you just give me?"

"A potion, sire."

"What kind of potion?"

Seris remained silent, darting his eyes away.

"Seris."

"It was never supposed to be made. I told the elders that it was too dangerous, but they insisted—."

"What is *it?*" Gods, why were the simplest questions always the most difficult to answer?

"Medicine. For your illness, sire."

What?

My eyes shot open like the city gates. "Why am I only hearing about this now? Hell, this feels more like a cure."

"It's not a cure." Seris bowed solemnly, "A cure was never possible to create."

"Then I'll ask again. Why am I only hearing about this now? This would have been very useful years ago."

Seris gasped as if the words had taken him hostage. "Because of the side effects."

"Oh," I said, stepping away from Seris.

Of course, there just had to be side effects.

What was it going to be? Mood swings? Sudden bodily combustion? Would I only be able to speak without vowels from now on?

The sorcerer sighed, wiping away a thick layer of sweat. He proceeded to take his glasses off and wipe them with his robes.

"The potion was a last resort in the case that the country needed you in a more..." Seris eyed the filth that was buried in my bed, "suitable state."

"Are the side effects deadly?" I asked, already suspecting Seris' next words.

He nodded, "Although the potion returns your health, it can only last for so long. With every dose, it will become less and less effective before eventually leading to..." He looked away.

"I understand." I patted Seris on the shoulder. Despite the secrecy, I could respect the man's intentions. "Will it lessen my time left?"

"Yes." The word came sharper than a sword, and trust me, I've had my fair share of those. "But with it, you'll be able to travel."

Suddenly, my eyes began to light up. "You mean I can actually leave? I'll be able to travel the country?"

"You will." This time, Seris smiled before passing. He cocked his head at me, giving my body the quick head-to-toe look over. "But, you won't be able to leave like that. Even though you've been ill for years, we can't afford to risk having you recognised."

"What do you propose?" I asked, intrigued by where Seris was going with this.

Without a word of warning, Seris began to conjure a spell, shifting his arms in a circular pattern, all the while muttering some gibberish that sounded like a foreign insult.

Speckles shined and shot out before the sorcerer's hands. His hair flared up as if a breeze had entered the room, voice echoing higher and deeper at once.

I took a step back, not knowing if I wanted to be near whatever Seris was conjuring. That is until he shouted. "Don't move!"

My body jolted upright.

"Please, sire. This spell is," Seris winced, "difficult."

I nodded.

Seris began to call out, all the while channelling whatever energy was inside him. It surrounded his body in several rings of blue starlight, orbiting around him.

"Seris?" I whispered as though speaking to my late wife during one of her episodes.

At once, all of the light shot out towards me, travelling instantly across the sorcerer, colliding with my chest.

My first instinct was to scream, and yet I felt no pain. Just a tingle of sorts. The light continued to shoot out into me, disappearing without a trace. Before long, all the light was gone. And all that was magical with Seris returned to normal.

"Umm, what was that supposed to...do." I stuttered at the last word, once again hearing a voice, unlike the one I possessed during my time of illness.

Seris was breathing rapidly, taking his time before responding. "I think it'll be easier to explain if I," Seris spun his hand within a blink of an eye, conjuring a mirror through thin air. He pointed at the closest candles in the room, emitting a flame from each one.

The room instantly grew brighter, and I began to walk towards the mirror, holding my breath with each step.

With every inch I got closer, I could see more and more of myself. Or rather, the face I was wearing.

"What the?" I cursed. I threw my hands to my face, ensuring that what I was seeing and feeling was the same. "A beard? Why are there so many blackheads? Gods, what are these thick eyebrows? Seris, what have you done to me now?"

"You mean, what have I done *for* you?" Seris patted his robes, removing a thick layer of dust and bits of glass. "It's a disguise spell. So long as you're with me, you'll be seen as this." He gestured to the mirror, which was now levitating. "If you're serious about travelling out there, about seeing the world before you die. Then this is how we'll do it, sire."

The face that was staring back at me was like most men. Young, hardened, but with a fair amount of soft spots. Of course, it had its unique qualities.

Yes, this could work.

"Okay, Seris. I'll confess you've outdone yourself. But I'll warn you, what we will do shall never be told to a living soul. Not to my son, nor any man in this kingdom."

Seris bowed. "You have my word, my king."

"And no matter what, you shall follow my every instruction along this journey. Should I tell you to run, you run. Should I tell you to strike me down, you must do so. Should I tell you to stop gawking at my magically impressive yet unattractive disguise," Seris eyes unfocused from my face, "you do so."

"Yes, sire. I understand." Seris nodded.

"Together, we'll head east. From there, we'll stop where I wish and camp out along the country. And most importantly," I tested the smile of my disguise, thankful that he had all of his teeth, "we'll have fun every moment we can find."

"Of course, sire." Seris nodded once more.

"And for the sake of the crown, don't call me sire. Or 'my king' or 'my liege.' If we're supposed to be hiding in plain sight, you'll have to call me something different for a change."

"I'll work on it, my—man?"

My face collided with the palm of my hand. Gods, this wasn't going to end well.

"So what now?" I asked, gazing around the room. What a mess, even without the destruction Seris had caused.

"Now," Seris sighed, extending his arm towards the stone-bricked wall across the room before waving. The wall pulled out, sliding to the side, revealing a lighted path within, "Follow that path until you reach the city's outskirts. From there, wait for me, and we'll begin this journey."

Was that there this whole time? I thought, wanting to ask Seris but knew he'd only give me the most complex answer. *Or maybe that was where they piled my years of filth.* I shivered at the image, hoping this was just an escape route and nothing else.

"What will you do?" I asked Seris, heading towards the pathway.

"Pack. How long did you say we would travel for?"

I shrugged, "Until I drop dead, I suppose."

Seris hummed, looking down as though calculating, "Yes, that will be quite a bit to prepare. Regardless, I will need to prepare my things. Gods know how much we'll need."

This was the part of Seris I admired. The way he was able to act so professionally, so deviously. It wouldn't matter if he couldn't conjure even a simple illumination spell. His mind was what set him apart at the university, and with it, a personal letter of recommendation.

I began to enter the hidden pathway until Seris tapped me on the shoulder.

"Just one last thing," he said before plucking a hair from my head. Immediately, it changed from the disguises bland brown to auburn. My hair's natural colour.

I winced, "Hey, what was that for?"

"For assurance. After all, we are faking your death. What better way than to disguise a corpse?"

"Are you saying..." I closed my mouth, shaking my head, "I don't want to know. Just get it done."

"I will." Seris bowed, "I'll meet you outside of the city." The sorcerer opened the chamber doors and left.

I knew then that Seris wanted to remind me that this was my last chance. To say goodbye, forget this plan, live the last of my time with my son, and prepare him for the future. But the truth was I had no intention of doing that. My son, in all my good faith, was as ready as he'll ever be. And as selfish as it may seem to say that I want to simply enjoy what little time I have left, well, this was one of the few times that I should be able to do just that.

A dying man should be able to do what he thinks matters.

And for me, I wanted to meet *her*.

Countrymen

The pathway ahead lurked with nothing but stone and cobwebs, leading into what felt like a never-ending maze.

To think that I never knew about this route or never saw anyone use it in my presence. Or perhaps they had while I was spiralling into a medically induced slumber.

I couldn't help but laugh as I continued. It was easy to forget that I was actually walking. After so many years in bed, I never thought I'd be able to do something as simple as wiggle my big toe. Now, here I was, travelling down an ongoing escape route, prepared for the journey to come. It was tempting to skip down the path, but then I decided I still needed some of my dignity.

I patted my pocket, ensuring that all I had taken was still there.

Pens and parchment. They were still there, along with the many letters I'd collected over the years. But Seris didn't need to know about that. He just had to keep me healthy until I found her.

I'm finally coming, Karness. Soon, we'll be able to meet. I just had to make sure I was headed in the right direction and got there before I was out of time.

After what felt like an hour, the line of torches stopped before a door.

"Finally," I said, rubbing my newly acquired legs. I'd almost forgotten what it was like to use my muscles—and to feel them grow tired.

I pushed the door open and was immediately touched by a cool night breeze. Praise the Gods, that felt like heaven. The only wind I'd felt in some time was, unfortunately, from my own making.

Apologies. But if I'm to bear that pain, so should you.

Despite how quickly my body began to shiver, I was happy to finally be out of the castle and the city. Judging from the plains before me, I was outside the eastern wall, just a couple of kilometres from the main road.

I stepped out the door, checking for any wanderers or furry beasts that might ambush me. I sighed in relief when I found I was alone, then turned around and gaped at what lay before me.

The city. I gawked at my home. Vilton, the capital I took from the usurpers so long ago.

The city rose and fell in several dips, stretching out in all directions with identical streets, broken only by the occasional structure that stood out. There was the grand cathedral—though I didn't visit much—the docks, the hall of healing, and the fighting bowl.

Hmm, that's new.

I squinted as I noticed a dragon standing atop a building, breathing fire against what looked like a smoky fillet. It was a wooden sign, of course, with the words 'The Dragon's Den' below it.

Must be a new restaurant chain, I thought. How long had that been there? And why was I never told about it? Sure, I wouldn't be able to eat anything as solid as a steak, but I could have at least been brought some fries, and maybe a toy.

Gods, I really missed out on a lot, didn't I?

Funny how time can change things.

I continued to gaze up at the city before laying eyes on the palace. It stood tall and as mighty as ever, lit like a beacon of light. It truly was a home for a king.

I smiled. *That's all yours now, son. Take care of it for me.*

"It's beautiful," a voice said.

I spun around and raised my fists, preparing for the fight of my life. Luckily, it was only Seris. Bloody bastard.

"Goddammit, Seris." I almost punched him, but considering he held the power to not only retain my disguised appearance but also to dampen my illness, I settled with only a gentle slap.

"I'm sorry, sire. I thought you could hear me coming."

This time, I flicked him on the nose as if I were shooing away an insect.

"Ow! What was that for?"

"Don't call me sire, Seris. Call me...call me Keltick."

"Keltick?" Seris asked, rubbing his nose. "Where did you get that name from?"

"What does it matter?" I tucked my hands into my pockets, feeling the smooth parchment of my letters. "Are we all packed?"

Seris rubbed his cheek. "We are. I left a note explaining that I needed to leave the city unexpectedly. No one, not even your son, should suspect anything."

"Very good." I nodded before tucking on my overshirt. "You wouldn't happen to have a spare coat on you, would you?"

Seris grinned, opening his robe before reaching into its pocket. He rummaged around inside it, poking his tongue to the side of his cheek. He stopped and at once pulled out a brown-fur coat.

"That's handy," I said.

Seris handed me the coat before closing his robe and patting it. "We've got everything we need. Food, water, camping supplies. All we need now is a direction."

"East," I said with no further explanation.

Seris pointed toward the open world. "Lead the way, Keltick." He winked.

I took one step forward before stopping. I turned around to see the city one last time. The evening nights were honestly a sight to behold. They each worked together to light the city so that all could see its majesty.

How have I never stood here before? Surely, I must have at some point in my life.

If I did, it must have been years ago.

"You coming?" Seris asked, sounding slightly concerned.

"Yes, I just...I want to have a look one last time." I stood there for nearly a minute, trying to memorise every detail I could find. Or perhaps it's because I knew that if I left, I'd never see this place again.

Come on. Move your ass. She's waiting for you.

I finally gazed away from the city. From my home. And everything and everyone I'd ever known. Well almost.

I took a step beside Seris and began heading toward the road. As we moved, I stopped for a moment, disheartened by the faint scent of what I could only imagine was some Dragon's Den fries.

The Catch of his Life

To answer your question, yes. I have always lived where I am now. Just south of the mountains in a small town by the coast. I've always wished to travel, but my body trembles whenever I grow tempted to leave. I'm sure you feel the same, Keltick.

But that isn't to say I don't enjoy where I live. Sure, there are some bad moments here and there, but such is the way of life. I'm happy where I am and would not be disappointed if this was where I had to be for the rest of my life.

I wouldn't know what to do if I were in the capital with you. My mind would probably scramble in the first hour.

Maybe that's why you began writing to me. Maybe you needed a little change in your life. Don't worry, I won't tell his majesty.

But in all seriousness, you should come here, Keltick. I'll show you everything my home has to offer. I could even take you fishing. We can head down to the docks and cast our lines out and cook whatever we catch. And don't you worry, I'll help you out if you've never fished before.

Do you civilised people even have fish over there? Have you ever seen a fish? Before it's been cooked, I mean?

My father used to take me out every day to fish. He always gave me the whole give a man a fish, and you'll feed him for a day spiel when I complained about not catching anything.

But that all changed one day. The day I caught my first bass and hauled it in with my dad.

I wish I could go back to that day with him.

I wish you could experience the joy it gifted me.

I gazed up from the parchment in front of me, unable to take away the smile from my face.

Tomorrow, we'll do just that.

"What's that?" Seris asked.

"Huh?" I tucked the letter away, clearing my voice. "Nothing. How's it coming along?"

"By *it,* you mean our tent?"

"Yes."

Seris' hands clapped together, creating a sharp sound that reverberated between him and me. In an instant, a room lined with linen and dark, crimson velvet appeared, stretching across ten square metres. The room instantly felt *comfortable,* as though we were completely resistant to any harm or irritation.

I don't know if that was because of Seris' magic or if the sight of velvet had just always succeeded in making me feel all the more elegant. But I made no effort to complain. There was no doubt that this was the most luxurious tent in the kingdom.

The room was lit with lanterns, dimmed to not harm our eyes nor keep us awake. Clever Seris. He'd also taken it upon himself to divide the illusive tent so that we slept in separate parts.

Although, now that I mention it, he could have at least created a spa of some kind. Heaven knows how long I've bathed without the need of a helper.

I nodded at Seris, genuinely impressed by his work. "So no one will know we're here?"

"No one. As far as anyone's concerned, we're just a couple of trees."

"Perfect." I yawned, "Well, this tree is about to timber. I suggest we both get some rest. Tomorrow will be a long day."

"It will? Why?"

"Because," I said, already falling face-first into my magically decorated King-sized bed, "we're going fishing."

I did not witness whatever peculiar twist of muscles Seris' face contorted, but I like to imagine it was how I felt when drinking medicine as a child. Actually, whenever I drank medicine, for that matter.

I say this because Seris' only response to my plan tomorrow was met with an unenthusiastic "eh." To which I silently but thoroughly enjoyed chuckling into my pillow.

The next morning began, and thus, so did the first day of the rest of my life.

For once, I awoke without the struggle to open my eyelids. My belly was no longer bloated and in need of immediate relief. At least for the first hour.

Yes, today was sure to be a fine day—one of the many ahead of my closing life.

In all honesty, the thought of death still felt foreign to me. It was like being in a race I never agreed to enter, one I couldn't ever picture myself finishing. Yet here I was, alive, moving my feet forward.

After a considerably delectable plate of bacon and eggs, Seris and I began to move on from our camp. We continued east, walking along the road like two simple travellers, though Seris couldn't help but stand out like a sore thumb—painted red with a sign that said, 'Yes, I am a sorcerer. Can't you tell from the robes?'

Luckily, we passed no curious folks, only some merchants happy enough to nod and greet us with a good morning.

I snickered, "Imagine their faces if they knew who we were."

"I'd rather not my—Keltick. We can't take any risks. Nor can we expect everyone we encounter to be decent. There's sure to be scum around these parts."

"Nonsense," I said. "The law has kept a tight control of these parts ever since I became king."

"Has it?" Seris asked.

"Of course," I said before considering. Surely, my kingdom hadn't fallen victim to such villainy during my reign. Yes, I wasn't exactly the most up-to-date on matters, but there hadn't been any reports brought to me. Had there?

"Crime and law are like a water wheel," Seris said. I could tell he was on the verge of saying, 'My king.' "Without one or the other, they cannot exist. Crime, no matter its country's ruler, can never *not* exist."

I inhaled each word as though it were air, holding them, considering the truth they possessed before exhaling. "I almost forget how wise you can be, Seris."

"Thank you, my liege."

At the last syllable from Seris' lips, I immediately kicked him in the shin.

"Ow!" Seris exclaimed.

"And then you remind me how clumsy you can be." I crossed my arms, watching my sorcerer rub at his leg.

"Fair point. But please, can you not kick me there? Another couple of those and I fear I won't be able to travel on."

"Sure." I sighed. "Sorry."

For the next hour, we continued with our travel, collecting gravel with our boots and kicking the occasional stone at a tree. I never realised how much fun a simple thing like that could be. Especially after Seris began to join in, and we kept score.

We stopped, though, just as he pulled ahead by two. How convenient.

We noticed a small cabin just a light walk away from the road, heading to a nearby stream.

Immediately, I smiled at the sight, knowing full well the day had just gotten better.

"What in all the Gods?" Seris said, appearing as if he couldn't make heads or tails about what lay before him.

Despite how well-researched the young sorcerer was, it was obvious he hadn't explored the *real* country. In truth, neither had I, but compared to a man whose head was neck deep in books, I felt that I had some advantage.

"It's a shop," I said, eyeing what had to be a 200-pound marlin hanging above the cabin's entrance.

"For what?"

I turned to Seris, hoping the face I was wearing appeared as cocky and somewhat conniving as I imagined. "Bait."

The cabin's front door jingled with a bell along its frame, causing Seris to jump and emit a light flame from his palms.

I, too, jumped, not because of the bell but because I was convinced Seris was about to light the cabin on fire. "Easy, Seris. It's just a bell."

"Apologies, my liege."

Now when I tell you that I was ready to slap the ever-living magical crap out of Seris, I mean it. Luckily for him, my violent attempt was interrupted by the cabin's shopkeeper, or at least that's who I assumed he was, based on the number of lures he had hanging from his pockets.

"Ho! Customers!" The shopkeeper's voice was muffled through his thick and nicely conditioned beard. Gods, why couldn't I ever grow such a thing? That right there was a King's beard.

The flames from Seris's palms extinguished within the blink of an eye, leaving only a hint of smoke from his fingertips. Immediately, the shopkeeper came charging towards us, testing the floorboards with his colossal physique.

He stopped just in time to avoid colliding with Seris and me, though I could have sworn I had moved an inch due to his belly nudging me.

"Hi. I'm Lerix." The shopkeeper said. "But you can call me Rix. My friends call me Rix."

Rix stuck his out hand at Seris, displaying his freshly made calluses. The sorcerer stuck his own out, taking the beast of a man's hand with good faith.

"Seris," Seris bowed, voice only slightly unnerved.

"And your name was..." Rix returned Seris' hand and turned to me with a bushy smile. "My liege?"

Oh no. My eyes darted like a crossbow bolt to Seris. I squinted at him with a look that said, 'Do something!'

"Ahh. Actually, it's pronounced 'Mileech.'" Seris scratched his head like how every lying brat did.

"Mileech?" Rix said, beating me by a second.

"Yeah. He's from the southern colonies. A foreigner. You know how odd their names can get over there."

I swear, Seris, I can never tell if you're a genius or a fool.

"Oh, right. Well, hey, welcome to the mainland, sir!" Rix took my hand and even wrapped his other around me, lifting me for a total of two seconds.

"Thank you," I said, surprised my spine hadn't popped out and caused me to collapse like I was made of jelly.

"So." Rix took Seris and me by the shoulder and walked us through his shop. To our left was an array of timber shelves laid against the wall, carrying numerous packets of worms, leeches, crickets and crayfish, all of which were still very much alive and moving. Opposite the bait was a rack of fishing rods, standing tall with rows of line, all ready to be cast into the water.

"What are two fine gentlemen such as yourselves doing in a place like this?" Rix asked.

"That's a good question." Seris eyed me. "What *are* we doing in a place like this?"

"Well, you see, my companion and I are planning to go fishing," I said, glad that Seris would be in no position to say otherwise.

"Fishing? Well, my friends, you've come to the perfect place." Rix gave us each a firm pat on the back.

Poor Seris. The man couldn't go a minute without being harmed.

"So what will you need, aye? Some bait? A net? A new rod? I know!" Rix charged behind his counter, rummaging through whatever was stored beneath. He threw behind him some line, a couple of bent fishing hooks, and even a harpoon.

Seris and I glanced at each other through the corner of our eyes.

"Aha!" Rix called out. He shot out from the depths of his counter, holding with him a hat that somehow looked big even for him. "A new hat!" The hat was made of straw and had a bright pink heart painted on the front.

"Umm," Seris began, appearing to consider igniting the shop, "we're actually in a rush, so we'll need to—."

"We'll take it!" I said, not at all wanting to wear the atrocious thing, but knowing it would stir Seris—especially once I made him wear it.

"Great!" Rix smiled and clapped his meaty palms.

"And we'll take one of those rods and some bait," I added.

"Mileech..." Seris hissed, nudging me in the ribs. "How will we pay for this?"

"With money," I said. "We have enough. Right?"

"We do. But I was under the impression that it would be used for the trip."

Rix looked back and forth between us as if we were fighting for custody.

"This *is* the trip, Seris." I narrowed my eyes at him, presenting one of my famous kingly stares. I always hated using it. It made me look like a wild animal, probably more so with this disguise. But I will admit it worked better than any magic when it came to getting things done. Or scaring the living hell out of people.

Seris proceeded to pull some coins from his pocket, "Fine." He slid them along the counter at Rix.

"Now," I clapped my hands and rubbed them, unable to contain my excitement. "Where's the nearest fishing spot?"

"I thought this would be more exciting," I said, sitting on the same damn rock for the last hour. So far, I hadn't felt anything as little as a tug on my line.

"Well, what did you expect? Fish don't just go leaping out by the dozens." Seris said, sitting comfortably against a tree as he read a book on enchantments. While he read, he wore the straw hat we had bought. From what I could tell, it had worked fairly well in blocking out the sun and even more so in making Seris appear all the more harmless.

"No. I just heard it was...different." I began to reel in my line, hoping that the next cast would do the trick.

Rix insisted that this lake was the perfect spot for fishing. It held a healthy current with plenty of depth and cover. The water itself was murky but not the worst I'd ever seen. Countless batches of reeds were protruding from the water like spikes, and the sun had just begun to descend, granting me a breathless sight.

The shopkeeper had also been kind enough to lock up the shop and guide us here, although I had a hunch that he hadn't had too much business lately. The man was far too keen to see to our needs. But then again, there was something about him that made the day brighter. His energy was frighteningly contagious and made you want to seize the day.

Maybe I should have got him to teach me how to cast a bloody line. Heavens know he wouldn't have refused.

"You know, if you really want a fish, I could always just cast a spell."

"No spells," I called out. "I want to do this right."

I finished reeling in the line, checking if the bait was still attached. "No bites," I sighed.

"The key is patience," Seris said.

"I gathered that. Any other tips?"

Seris shook his head, turning to a new page. "If you want, I can transform myself into a fish and tell them you mean no harm."

"Very fun...wait, you can do that?"

Seris nodded.

"Gross."

I readied my rod, pulling it back behind me, ensuring that it hadn't caught onto my pants. The last thing the fish needed was the sight of me in my undergarments. I counted down, exhaling with each number.

Three.

Two.

One.

I cast my line out, creating a thin line across the sky.

Come on. Come on. Give me something good.

It finally fell and touched the water, creating a ripple that spread in all directions.

But as I watched the ripple approach, a sudden spasm struck at my core. Weakness spread through my legs, then to the rest of my body. I tried to breathe but could do nothing but cry out in pain.

"Ahh," I exclaimed, unprepared for whatever was happening. "Seris!" I cried out.

"Oh no." Seris threw his book away. He bolted towards me with a vial in hand, already pulling the cork off.

By now, I was lying against the same rock by the lake, trying my best not to scream any more than I had. Somehow, I still held on to the fishing rod, gripping it as if it would dampen the pain. "Seris!"

"I'm here, Deveric." He held up my head, taking the vial and pouring its contents into my mouth. "Drink, sir. Drink."

I did, and after there was no more to drink, I lay there, gasping for breath. "Th...thank you." I sat up, body now drenched in sweat.

"What was that?" I asked between breaths.

"The illness..." Seris said with certainty; however, his eyes lingered with complete and utter shock. "It wasn't supposed to return this quickly."

I continued to take deep breaths, calming my rapid heart. "How long was it supposed to last?"

"A week, give or take."

I stared at Seris for a handful of seconds. "It's been two days. Wait, no. It's been less!"

Seris shook his head. "I swear I calculated it precisely to last a week, minimum. How could..." The sorcerer's head fell like an executioner's axe. "Seris, you idiot."

I cocked an eyebrow, waiting for whatever explanation the supposed idiot was about to give.

"I measured the potion to your conditions when you were back in Vilton," Seris sighed. "Back when all you did was lie in bed."

I recoiled, my head snapping back. "I did a lot more than that, thank you very much."

"My point is," Seris raised a palm, "that I expected this potion to last a week on an *inactive* individual. I never considered how long it would last for someone roaming the country.

Oh. That would explain it.

I sat myself up, taking in this new information. "That was...painful." Had I not almost died, I would've begun snickering at the large pink heart on Seris' hat.

Seris nodded. "The illness returns more severely each time."

You don't say. I rubbed at my temple. How many times would I be able to survive these...attacks? Especially now that they were going to be so frequent?

Seris patted me on the back. "Come on, sire. We should ready ourselves for camp."

For a second, I considered his words. After all, today had been, for one thing, eventful.

But eventful didn't necessarily mean exciting.

"Okay," I said.

But suddenly, I felt something pulling on me. I thought it was another recurrence of my illness, but that's until I looked down at the rod in my hand.

Something was pulling on the line.

"Seris! Seris! I..." I stammered, excitement taking over. "Fish!"

Seris' eyes darted at the rod, then at me. "Hold onto it! Don't let it get away! Reel it in!"

I gripped the rod with my other hand. For a second, it felt like I was holding a longsword, ready for battle. I began to reel in the line, over and over and over, fighting with the monster at the end. It began tossing and turning within the water, leaving only the very faintest traces of its position.

"Come on. Come on. Come to me." I said, struggling to hang on.

"You got this, sire!"

I used every ounce of strength I had in my body to hold on to the rod. There was no chance in hell that this fish was going to win today. Either the fish was coming to land, or I was going to go swimming. Perhaps I should have purchased that harpoon as well.

Finally, the fish began to slow down, tired from its protests.

"Now!" Seris called out like he was couching me.

I spun my reel over and over again, bringing my prize closer to me. "Almost there," I said with gritted teeth. I could see its body through the murky water.

"Gods above." Seris squinted through his lenses, eyeing my prize.

I made one last rotation before reaching for the line and pulling out the body of a beast. It flapped around like my tongue after a spicy meal.

Fight all you want, big guy. You're not going anywhere.

I turned to Seris, waiting for him to say something. Instead, he just laughed, and soon enough, I joined in before kissing my first catch.

A Song and a Drink

Dear Keltick,

What do you do for fun? I ask because you never tell me what you do in your spare time. Do you go for walks, do you like to draw? Does the king ever give you time off to enjoy life?

For me, I like to sing.

My mother used to sing to me before she passed, from the time I was a babe until I was about nine. She had a soothing voice that always made me fall asleep. Granted, she wasn't the best singer, but if you had heard her voice, you would agree that it was a gift from the Gods.

One of my favourites was this one called 'A New Day.'
It went like this:
A new day has come,
A new day has started.
Yesterday has gone,
Yesterday has parted.
And so we must move on,
And so we must be kind-hearted.
For today is a new day,
Now listen to what I have to say.

I know what you're thinking. Pretty simple and uncreative. But there's something about it that feels nostalgic to me, that reminds me no matter what, tomorrow will bring something new.

Maybe it's also because most times I hear this song, I've had a couple of beers already and am surrounded by intoxicated sailors.

Not to say this happens regularly—I only drink on rare occasions. But when I do, it always brings out my singing

The sun had decided to slumber by now, and Seris had created our tent once again. With it, he generated a fire pit and a filtration system so that we didn't suffocate from smoke. Or from the smell of cooking fish.

Atop the fire pit was a cast iron pan, holding within it the fish I had caught.

"Gods, it gets bigger and bigger every time I look at it," I said, licking my lips.

"A mighty fine catch, sir. Mighty fine." Seris lifted his hand palm side up, fuelling the fire with his sorcery.

"What kind is it?" I asked, possessing little to no knowledge of fish and the types that existed.

"A bass." Seris poked at it with a spatula. Gods, how many things did that robe of his carry? "Should be ready soon," he said.

"Great," I fell into a cushion, listening as the fish sizzled in the pan.

Today had been fun. Despite the potion's effects wearing off, today had been memorable. Maybe the most memorable day for me in some time. Then again, literally anything was better than staying in Vilton's palace. Lying in bed, tormented by relentless coughing while struggling to digest even a simple meal like soup. What a bleak existence that was.

At least now I had a glimpse of finding a fulfilling end to my life. I just hoped that my time wouldn't slip away too quickly.

"What are you thinking of?" Seris eyed me.

I shrugged. "Nothing, why?"

"You're smiling is all."

"Huh?" I felt at my face, the disguise's face that is, and was shocked to realise that he was right.

I guess I am.

"So, what's our plan for tomorrow?" Seris asked, "Not more fishing, I hope."

"Tomorrow," I took a moment to consider, as well as inhale the mild smell of the bass. "I suppose we'll travel and see what the day brings us."

Seris nodded, turning back the pan. "Sir. I don't mean to be blunt—."

"And yet you're about to be."

The sorcerer sighed, lifting the fish to ensure it hadn't been burnt and was cooking evenly. "I can't help but wonder why we are travelling. Or where we're travelling to, for that matter. Not to mention those letters you've been reading."

My body immediately tensed as he mentioned the letters.

So he's noticed. Of course, he had. Sorcerers always like to stay informed, even if it doesn't involve the latest discoveries in magic or alchemy. They were naturally nosy people, for better or worse.

So far, I had only read Karness' letters during this expedition at times when I thought I had privacy. Usually, I would pull them out after Seris had fallen asleep or was occupied by his own reading material. Had Seris been pretending? Or was he using some sort of spell?

"Don't worry, I haven't been spying on you, sire. I'm just saying that you shouldn't keep things from me, especially in these next few weeks." Seris' eyes lowered, touching on the fact that my time was drawing closer to its end.

My 'attack' today had been a painful reminder of that, but Gods, I'd have to go through much worse if it meant I could find Karness and speak to her for a minute.

Before the end.

"You're a good man, Seris. And I'm thankful that you agreed to come with me. But if these truly are my last weeks alive, then I'll decide what we will and won't do."

For a moment, Seris' face became twisted with frustration, tightening around his chin and forehead. But then he relaxed, exhaling with a breath that flowed gently through the tent like the night's wind. "Very well." He levitated the pan off the fire. "That should do,"

I smiled. "Looks like a meal fit for a king."

"Okay, your turn now," I said to Seris.

We had just crossed a stone bridge along the main road and were asking each other random questions to pass the time. So far, I was asked about my time during the uprising and shared a couple of war stories and violent anecdotes that Seris failed to find as amusing as me. Seris, on the other hand, told me about how, one time, an experiment he did at the university resulted in the invention of mayonnaise. However, he continued by explaining that he was caught in the middle of a conspiracy and thus was not credited for the revolutionary condiment.

Personally, I was more of a fan of tomato sauce, but I enjoyed the story all the same.

"Hmm," Seris tapped at his chin. "If you had to be reborn as an animal, what would you be?"

"What kind of question is that?" I asked, furrowing my brows.

"An honest one. You're telling me you've never thought of what it would be like to be a bird? Or a dog?"

"Well, considering I've never been able to transform into an animal, unlike someone I know, then yes, I've never considered it."

Seris hummed to himself, "Touché."

We continued for another minute, now surrounded by nothing but curved willow trees and a road stretching into the distance. You wouldn't think it was afternoon under the cover of the forest, but then again, that was one of its powers—it could swallow all light and leave its guests perplexed.

Luckily, my accompanying sorcerer was able to emit an illuminated pathway for us.

"So?" Seris leaned over to me.

"What?"

"You given it any thought yet?"

I rolled my eyes until I noticed a couple of squirrels chasing each other along a tree branch.

"What animal lives the longest?" I asked, still staring at the two squirrels.

Seris followed my gaze, seeming to understand. "A phoenix. The longest recorded lifespan of one is said to be over five hundred years old."

"Five hundred years," I whispered.

"Of course, there can only be one phoenix existing at a time."

I turned to Seris, astounded.

"It's true. Phoenixes are incredible creatures. But that's the price for their existence." He paused, cocking his head at me before eyeing the pair of squirrels. "Do you reckon you could be one?"

Having spent years alone in my chambers, I'm surprised I lasted as long as I did. Each day was a struggle, blending one eternity after the next. If I had to relive it, I'm not sure I'd have the strength to do so. Sure, loneliness had become a good friend at that time, but that isn't to say I invited it with open arms.

How could a creature live for so long without anyone?

I gazed back at the squirrels, but before I knew it, they were gone. "No," I said. "No, I don't think I could."

We walked for another hour before reaching the end of the Willow Tunnel, as it was infamously named. From there, Seris and I were left with nothing but endless hills of green and wooden fences.

The light of day was nearly gone, and so Seris and I began to slow down and prepare for camp. But that was until we heard it.

"What is that?" I asked, spinning in all directions.

"There." Seris pointed along the top of a distant hill. There was a building emitting just barely enough light. Seris and I stood still, listening.

"It sounds like...cheering," I said.

"And singing," Seris added. "Must be a tavern for travellers." He turned back, raising his hands to prepare the camp.

"Maybe we should check it out," I proposed, trying my best not to sound overly eager.

"Check it out?" Seris gawked at me with his perfectly round glasses. "Why? So we can end up getting knocked out and having our possessions stolen?"

"Do you really hate crowds that much? Come on, from what it sounds like, it could be fun. Plus, I can't remember the last time I had a drink." Seris began to raise his finger, ready to retort. "And no, that doesn't mean I want to drink whatever concoction you've made."

For all I know, it'll taste like mayo.

The tavern wasn't too far from where we were. Of course, Seris had complained along the way and was winded by the time we reached the top of the hill.

As we neared, the ensemble of cheers and harmonious echoes rose louder within our ears.

"Sounds like a full night tonight," Seris commented. "I guess we won't be able to go in." He began to turn around, but I quickly seized him by his collar and gave him a slight but firm pull.

"Quit being a wuss, Seris," I said while heading to the entrance. "Let's live a little."

"Easy for you to say," I heard Seris mumble.

I pushed open the tavern's front door and was immediately blasted with radiance and uproar. It was as though the room itself was alive, fresh from a long slumber. Every seat and table was taken, and with it was a mug for each man and woman.

"Gods," Seris' voice was drowned out by the crowds. He drew close to me, closer than most ever got to a king. "Sir, I *really* think we should get out of here."

"Hush. We're not in trouble yet, Seris." It was odd to test the capabilities of this body's voice. "And remember, call me Keltick."

I eyed a couple of men leave the bar. "Come on," I said to Seris.

We headed to the free spots and sat down, relieved that no one had beaten us to them.

"Must be an occasion?" I leaned over to Seris, eyeing the amount of customers.

"We're drinking to the king," a rather young but rough-looking man said beside me. "Man finally died just two days before. Orders are to celebrate and drink to his name." He took a sip of his mug, exhaling after he swallowed. "Not that I need a reason for a cold drink, you understand me?"

I nodded, "I do." I raised my brows at Seris, unable to suppress a grin. "I suppose we ought to join in and drink to his majesty's honour. What are you drinking, friend?" I asked the man.

"Ale."

"Excuse me," I signalled for the bartender, "three ales please." I nodded at the man beside me, thankful that he returned one.

"What?" Seris asked. "Keltick, with all due respect—."

I leaned over to Seris and hissed, "Don't worry. I'll make sure you're compensated for this."

"It's not that," the sorcerer explained. "It's just that I don't like...Ale. I was hoping for something more...rich."

I rolled my eyes, looking at the bartender like an embarrassed child. I almost said to him, 'I'm not with this man. I've never met him in my life.'

"Don't worry," I patted him on the shoulder, "one drink, and we'll head back out. Okay?"

Seris' mouth opened like a draw bridge, ready to protest. Instead, he snapped it shut and said, "Okay."

Another minute passed before our drinks arrived. They stood tall in a wooden mug, each holding a fresh head of creamy froth, all the while filling our nostrils with a fruity aroma.

I had to wipe my mouth quickly so as not to spill drool on the bar. I lifted the mug, waiting for Seris to join me in a toast.

"To Deveric Johanis, the late king," I said, neck shivering as I spoke my name out loud.

Seris raised a brow at me. "To a good man."

Our mugs collided with one another, causing a slight spill on my behalf. I sipped at the mug, allowing the cold liquid to quench my thirst.

"Ahhhh," I sighed, satisfied. "Best drink I've ever had."

"Mmm," Seris tapped on his belly, "delicious."

"Mmhmm. Taste a lot like cherries." I said, eyeing Seris as I took another sip.

Seris took the mug to his mouth, holding it for a second too long. "It does."

"Aha," I called out, a little too loudly. "You haven't even tasted it yet. It tastes nothing like cherries."

Seris grimaced as I caught his lie. Before he could respond, however, he paused and turned in his seat.

Everyone in the room was quiet, eyeing Seris like he was fresh meat.

Whoops, I thought.

"Drink it," I whispered to him.

"Drink it." The words echoed through each patron. They chanted like they were performing a ritual. "Drink it. Drink it. Drink it. Drink it."

After what felt like an eternity, Seris finally raised his mug and slowly but hesitantly brought it to his lips. He left it there for a total of two seconds.

Everyone, including myself, leaned in and watched as Seris gulped the drink before removing the mug and revealing a frothy moustache.

The room exploded with cheers and applause, reverberating through the chairs. I, of course, joined in the ludicrous scene, slamming my fist repeatedly against the bar like a barbarian.

Intoxicated, not by the drink but by the crowd, Seris continued to drink, swallowing with each mouthful. With the last gulp, he slammed the mug down, producing the most profound hiccup I had ever heard. And that's saying something coming from me.

"Attaboy," I said as I patted Seris. "Bartender, could you get this man some water, please." The last thing I needed was for Seris to become drunk and begin showcasing his latest set of destructive spells.

"Sure thing," the bartender smiled before pouring a mug.

Slowly, the room fell back into its previous state, murmuring about whatever was going on with their lives.

"I..." Seris let out a violent hiccup, "am never doing that again."

I snickered, "Not tonight you are. That's for sure."

Before I could thank the barkeeper as he brought Seris his water, the room began to louden once again. Only this time, they didn't cheer or chant. Their voices were melodious, speaking in a rhythm that was strange yet all too familiar.

"They're singing," I said to myself rather than to Seris or anyone around.

"Mmhmm," Seris hummed between sips of water.

"Seris. If I join in, do you swear not to abandon me?"

Seris nodded, bobbing his head like it was weightless.

"Good man," I patted him on the back. "Bartender. If it wouldn't be a hassle, I would very much appreciate it if you could look after my friend for me."

The man was drying a mug with a cloth, eyeing me with a tight grin. He nodded, "Consider it done."

My smile stretched from ear to ear as I headed towards the singing group. They were singing a song about the king, praising him and saying how they would drink all night in his honour.

As they should.

I neared the group and watched as they turned to me, voices still singing while their eyes hardened. In a flash, they each brightened as they waved me over as though I were a long-lost friend.

If you asked me, it was probably because they each had a trio of empty mugs on their tables. But I didn't mind that. These people were enjoying the night, and so was I.

The group and I huddled together like brothers in arms, beginning the same song they'd been singing moments ago. Only now, they sang it louder and far less comprehensibly.

Now, now where's the crown?
Under the mound, atop the town.
Now, now how's the crown?
Not a sound. Not even frown.
The crown, crown goes around.
Up and down. Round and round.

The song continued to loop over and over, becoming slightly repetitive but amusing all the same. *If only they knew,* I thought.

New Day, Same Pain

"Ow," I groaned. My eyes struggled to open like a stubborn envelope.

Everything hurt, and not because I needed another dose of Seris' medicine, but because last night had ended abruptly—and most likely with me 'refunding' my drinks.

I licked my lips, catching the scent of my breath. Yep, I had definitely refunded last night.

I sat up, feeling the world spin in a dozen different directions. *Gods, if you're real, please show me mercy.*

They did not.

Fortunately, they were decent enough to prevent me from spewing again. At least not outside of my mouth.

I rubbed my head, wishing this was all over.

But while I sat, waiting for the rush of the new day to hit me like a battering ram, I began to remember last night—the cheering, the drinking, the singing. Gods, the singing. We must have sung until the roosters crowed. Or until we all collapsed on the floor.

Poor Seris. The man must have had to—.

"Seris!" I turned around and saw only a small room with a bed and table. Where the hell was I? This couldn't be our camp, could it? Not unless Seris had downgraded his interior designs.

"Seris!" I called again. Still nothing.

"Dammit, dammit, dammit." I began to get dressed, readying myself for however long it was going to take to find Seris.

What if he was abducted? What if a strange man who runs a circus took him while I wasn't looking?

I could already imagine Seris juggling balls of fire while wearing a motley. Gods above. No one steals my sorcerer.

I burst forth from the room, scanning the hallway with my fists raised. It had been over a decade since I'd been in combat, let alone a fistfight, but that isn't to say that I'd forgotten how to throw a punch.

I inched myself forward to the other end of the hall, preparing for anyone or anything to pop out from the doors on each side.

This must be some sort of haunted mansion. Possessed by all types of devils and witchery.

How was I supposed to fight?

I paused, feeling a sudden build-up of gas rise to my throat.

Oh gods.

Now I had two options here. Neither of which was ideal. Do I burp and therefore alert everyone here? Or do I risk imploding?

My body decided for me, causing the walls to vibrate and test their structural integrity.

"Okay," I whispered to myself. "Time to focus, Deveric."

At the end of the hallway, a set of stairs stood, spiralling down to what I hoped was the ground floor. Not one part of me today, both in and out, wanted to take any more stairs than was needed. But dammit, I had a man to save.

I descended the steps slowly, reaching the last with ease. I sighed, catching the scent of myself again.

Before I continued, I began to hear groans coming from ahead. Painful, agonising groans. Oh no. I leaned forward, hoping to hear some indication of what I would be up against. I began to hear...laughing?

What sick devilry was occurring here?

I leaned against the wall, shaking my head every time I instinctively reached for a sword. Hell, I would kill for at least a dagger. Oh well, fists would do. Perhaps I would be able to have a warrior's death after all this time.

I sighed, taking in a deep breath before jumping out like a sleep-deprived maniac, ready to destroy all in my way.

I jumped outwards but stopped as I caught sight of what was in front of me. People. Normal people. Simply sitting and enjoying a new day. Some were groaning while next to a bucket, while others had a cup of steaming tea in their hands. Others were fast asleep, smiling like they'd just been sung a lullaby.

And in the midst of this was Seris, alive and well, if not slightly drowsy.

"Good morning," he said while handing a cup of tea to an old, rugged individual who, judging from the colour of his beard, had had a few too many mugs last night.

"Ah, hi," I lowered my fists, pretending they were in my pockets the whole time. "What's going on?"

Seris rolled his eyes within those giant glass discs, sighing exhaustively. "Well, after your brilliant performance last night and a couple of hours of hydrating myself beside a quiet tree, I returned to find this." He gestured around the room and its unfortunate occupants. "After I put you to bed, which I paid for," he squinted at me fiercely, "I began seeing to every poor soul here."

Like a badly timed joke, a boy, fresh off the ship called 'manhood,' began to cover his mouth, trying desperately to prevent a spillage.

"Gods above," Seris whined, "Theodore, we talked about this. Run outside before—."

Unfortunately, Theodore didn't make it out on time. Instead, he made a mess that I suspect Seris was feeling obligated to clean.

Despite how Seris' eye twitched at me, and how the smell of fresh vomit was now travelling to my nose or the fact that my head still felt like a hamster on a wheel, except the hamster was dangerously obese and the wheel had been closed for maintenance, I couldn't help but smile.

At everything. At nothing.

I was on the floor, giggling like a toddler, feeling tears of untapped glee stream down my cheeks.

Never in my life did I ever suspect to find such...such...what was the word? Happiness? No. That word was too generic and useless in describing what I felt now.

Whatever it was, it was a combination of being half asleep with a full bladder, all the while remembering a night that I'd remember until—.

Until.

I paused my wild laughing fit, taking a moment to catch my breath before rising from the floor. "Seris," I muttered, "we should get going."

The young sorcerer gawked at me for a moment. But then he sighed and nodded as if remembering why we were *really* here. "Very well."

For some reason, every step we took afterwards felt a little harder than before, like my boots were filled with stones, sinking into the earth. The only thing that kept them moving, one after the other, was that I still had to see *her*.

If I could figure out where she was.

"What's got you in the sulk?" Seris asked, despite not turning in my direction.

"Nothing," I lied. "Just recovering."

Seris hummed. "You know I can cure that for you. Dampening migraines is one of the first spells they teach at the university, you know."

"Good to know," I winced, feeling my head thump, "But being that this is the first hangover I've had in over a decade, I don't want to see it go away so soon."

That was enough to make Seris turn to me. He eyed me as though I'd just said, 'Magic isn't real.'

"You continue to surprise me, sire." He snapped his fingers, bringing with it a wave of ease to both my mind and body.

Cheeky bastard.

"So where are we off to next, Keltick?" Seris said the name mockingly.

"Ahh," I gazed ahead at the trail. "There's a town not far ahead. We'll stop there for the night."

"What's there?"

"Why does it matter?"

"Well, the last stop we made, you left me alone so you could get drunk and sing your little heart out. I think it's only fair I know what's to come next."

I had to pinch myself, checking to see if I were dreaming. If I were, at least I would have some sort of explanation on why Seris was in such a mood. But then again, he did have a point.

That doesn't mean I had to tell him the truth. Did it?

I swallowed. "There's a Dragon's Den there. A man at the tavern told me about it. I thought we could go there and treat ourselves to a nice meal."

Seris stopped in his tracks, his mouth almost dropping to the damp ground. "A Dragon's Den? Really?"

"Yep. Of course, I don't know if he was telling the truth, but I figure we can check out the town, regardless."

"Sounds like a plan," Seris smiled, a little too brightly for my liking. "And maybe after, we can go for a stroll. Maybe treat ourselves to a manicure. Or better yet, we can see if there's a tourney happening. Or, or, hear me out, we can have you enlist in one." Seris began to spread his arms out like he was imagining a billboard. "King Deveric, local jousting champion."

I exhaled, long and hard, until my lungs were practically empty. I glanced to my side and found a boulder to lie beside, not wanting to stand while whatever was about to happen happened.

"Okay, Seris," I said, glad but somewhat irritated that my headache was gone. "You made your point. Now out with it."

Seris' body began to shake, starting from his hands and spreading to his arms and then the rest of his body. It was most pronounced, however, in his face, as if he couldn't contain what he was about to say.

Please don't light me on fire, Seris.

The veins on his neck and forehead were thumping, reminding me of my fellow comrades during the war. Only now, I was far more frightened, surprisingly.

"I've had enough of your lies, dammit!" Seris' voice echoed across the land, bouncing off each stone, tree and hill across a hundred kilometres.

Before I knew it, my heart was racing, not because I was afraid but because—.

"Oh no," I said, clutching my chest, feeling a jolt of incoming pain.

"You're not telling me everything! You keep dragging me along with you, like, like I'm some sort of pet. Why? Why are we out here?"

The pain was spreading throughout my body like lightning, tingling every nerve with a hot knife. Gods, make it stop. Make it stop.

"Seris," I whimpered. "Please."

I curled myself into a ball, hoping it would lower the pain's intensity. It didn't.

"Seris," my voice was fading fast. It wouldn't be long before I lost all strength and consciousness. "Please. Please. Help me...Karness!"

Everything turned to black. I could still feel the pain, though even that was beginning to fade. All that remained was darkness. It faded slowly into a darker shade, like a starless night, although no aspect redeemed how cold it felt or appeared. It extended into eternity and I began to feel lost. Forever.

"My liege! My liege! Come on Deveric! Wake up!"

My eyes shot open, waking to see nothing but sky and flared nostrils that were in great need of trimming.

"Gods above," I groaned, feeling at my chest. The pain was completely gone. I gave my lips a lick. The potion. "You saved me," I peered at Seris.

"Of course," the sorcerer gave a weak smile. "Sorry for before. I didn't realise—."

"It's okay." My head was sweating profusely. How long had I been out? I stared at my hands, trying to open them slowly without shaking. It felt as though all my motor functions were dulled like I'd lost all prior experience.

This illness. To think I spent a quarter of my life suffering from this. And now I had come close to death from it, not once but twice.

"I thought I was gone there," I said.

"Me too," Seris sighed. "The potions' effects are dulling."

"The next one will come sooner, won't it?" I knew the answer but asked regardless.

He nodded. Dammit. How much time did we have left? A day? Two days?

Seris and I sat there along the trail for a minute, catching our breaths and digesting what had happened. *Now would definitely be a good time to set up camp,* I thought.

"Sir?" Seris spoke. "Who's Karness?"

Crap. My eyes opened like Vilton's city gates.

What do I say? Do I tell him she was an old fling during my younger days? No, he wouldn't believe that not for a second.

Dammit, it was time to come clean, wasn't it?

I sighed, knowing this was going to take some time to explain. "Let's set up camp first. Then, I'll tell you all you wish to know."

The Truth

It began not long after the illness had started. At this time, I could still walk and move as usual, but I decided it was best to confine myself to my chambers. At least then, I wouldn't have to face the constant stares of the nobility and my son.

So, while I remained in my chambers, gathering phlegm and all other types of substances, I saw to my royal duties.

On a good day, my desk would be piled with letters close to my shoulder height. When I sat down, that is.

Unfortunately, that day was not today.

Letters from all over the kingdom assembled before me, making my quill squirm with nervousness. Luckily, my hands were still useful, and I had all the time in the world.

I started by dividing each letter into separate groups: one for general inquiries, another for plantation reports, taxes, harvests, crime—you name it.

When people imagined a king, they envisioned a man wearing a majestic crown, with servants offering him berries while he sat upon a mountain of rubies and gold. Few, however, realised the true nature of the job—or that it was, in fact, a job at all. It was a responsibility, a burden that few could ever truly understand.

Each pile of letters stood taller than the next, awaiting me to open them and read their contents. There were only a handful of letters left to organise; however, I stopped and paused as one stood out before me.

At first, I thought my mind was playing tricks with me, being that I had been at my desk for some hours and was beginning to see all the letters blend into one. But no. My eyes were functioning perfectly. The letter in front of me didn't hold the same coffee-stained off-brown that most had. Nor did it have any wax to seal it. Instead, there was a thin rope tying the paper together tightly, but not too tightly, so that it would cause damage.

"What the?" I said, turning the letter over each side.

On its face, the letter held a drawing of the sea, with a man rowing a boat against a crashing wave.

I pursed my lips, eyeing the details.

Good colouring. Although it could use something to spice it up. Maybe a shark or some lightning in the background.

But that wasn't all that made the envelope stand out. There was another drawing, now on the back. And with this one, I could not complain.

It was a crown, a gorgeous, brilliant, golden crown atop a red velvet cushion. It floated at the envelope's centre.

Damn. Why didn't my crown look that good?

To open this and destroy such beauty was almost a crime, but by now, I confess, I was beyond curious about what was inside.

I winced as I untied the rope and opened the envelope with my paper-knife. I'd have to store this one somewhere safe if I could. Inside was a single piece of parchment, once again holding beautiful illustrations, this time of birds and green mountains on each side.

I smiled at the drawings, brushing them with my fore-finger. Whoever wrote this had obviously put a lot of work into it. That had to be a good enough reason for me to read it before all of the rest.

I began to read the letter.

To his majesty, King Deveric Johanis,

Good morning or evening, Your Majesty. I wasn't sure when you would be given this letter or whether it would ever reach you. The postal service here is terrible so I suspect this was lost in a storm some weeks ago.

But on the off chance it wasn't, and on the 'offer' chance it was able to reach you, I'd like to take my time and say thank you.

I furrowed my brows at that. What was I being thanked for?

Ever since you came to power, my town has thrived dramatically. No longer have there been days where we lay hopeless, starved and forgotten. Because of you, our lands have grown stronger and our people happier.

Most people here would argue it was purely coincidental, that things simply had become more fortunate as time went on. But I know better. Because of you and the peace you've brought to this land, we are alive.

I know this may not mean much to you, being that you're a king and must hear this sort of thing all the time. But I just wanted to say that we appreciate you. I appreciate you and all you've done for this kingdom.

Thank you for taking the time to read this and I will understand if you are unable to reply.

Kind regards, and warm welcomes,

Karness.

P.S. I hope you enjoyed the drawings. My father said they were a tad childish but I figured they would help make my letter stand out.

P.P.S. I hope you feel better soon.

The letter ended there.

"Karness," I whispered to myself. The name rolled on the tongue so easily. I said it out loud again, pronouncing each syllable slowly.

I read the letter again, taking my time with each sentence, trying to imagine the woman who'd written it. For some reason, I pictured a young, short-haired brunette with an oval face. Her lips were full, and she had a fair complexion with a few freckles across her cheeks. I don't know why I imagined this, but when I read the name Karness, that was what came to mind.

Of course, I'd have preferred to see her in person, but the likelihood of that happening was next to none.

While I read the letter again, I eyed one of the last written lines.

I will understand if you are unable to reply.

Those words sunk inside of me like my morning pills. This woman had gone out of her way just to thank me, to tell me how appreciative she was. The least I could do was reply to her and tell her how much her words meant to me.

But that couldn't happen. I was the king, and the king didn't have time to reply to every person in the realm.

Except Karness wasn't like every person in the realm. Not to me. Despite how little I knew of her, there was something about her words that sparked inside of me that made my time in isolation feel just that little less painful.

But I was the king. I had duties to attend to. I had a pile of letters to open and read.

If I wasn't the king, I would—.

I stepped away from my desk, holding my chin, contemplating my next move as if I were playing a game of chess.

I pulled open a drawer from my desk. No envelopes. Damn.

"Guards!" I called towards my door. At once, two men wearing armour from head to toe with a sword and shield came charging in.

"My king, are you alright?" One of the men asked.

"We heard you shout." The other said.

"I'm fine, I'm fine. I just need one of you to get me some parchment and envelopes, is all." I began to cough, turning away from the guards.

"Of course, my liege." The guards performed a salute and nodded.

"We'll have someone grab those at once." One of the guards left, while the other remained in my quarters.

"Good, good," I said, wiping my mouth with a handkerchief.

"Are you alright, my liege?" The guard asked.

"I am, thank you. It's nothing." I sighed. There was some blood on the handkerchief, more than usual. Great.

"Would you like me to get one of the doctors?"

"No, no. I'm fine. I just...I just need some parchment." The guard nodded.

I eyed the man carefully. He was young, at least twenty-five, from what I could see behind his helm. He'd been here for around a year now, although it was hard to tell, considering how little I saw my guards.

"What's your name, son?" I asked.

"Keltick, sir." He said proudly.

"Keltick. Hmm, that's a nice name."

"It means to wish," Keltick said, maintaining his posture. I wouldn't have asked him for the meaning, but I'm glad he mentioned it.

The other guard returned with a full stack of paper and envelopes. He placed it atop my table before exiting the room with Keltick. They shut the doors behind them, leaving their king alone once again.

Except, I wasn't alone. Nor was I the king.

I strolled to my desk, taking a seat before dipping my quill into some ink.

Where do I start? I read the last third of Karness' letter, trying to figure out a worthy reply. I began to scratch at a fresh piece of parchment, decorating it with strokes of ink.

"Dammit," I said as I made an error. How do you spell 'exstatik' again? Ex? Ec? Ecstatic? Surely, that was the right way to write it.

"This is going to take some time." Had this been any other letter regarding either taxes, building permits or any other boring political aspect, my reply would've been taken away for review by my scribes to check for overall spelling and grammar. From there, it would be made more 'kingly' before being sent out.

But with this letter, I knew I could not let anyone read it or know this was from me.

And so, with that, I started again. And again. And again. Until I was satisfied with what I'd written.

I flatted out the paper, gazing along the lines carefully.

Dear Karness,

I am happy to inform you that your letter has indeed reached the capital, and in addition, has been read by His Majesty himself.

As you can tell, I am not the King, Deveric Johanis.

My name is Keltick, and I am one of the king's scribes, employed to oversee the comings and goings of his letters.

I will confess, upon receiving your letter, I took it upon myself to open it and read what was inside. Forgive me, but I was too curious not to open it. The illustrations and designs are unlike anything I've ever seen in my years here.

In regards to the king, he was very pleased by your thankful words and has asked me to write to you while he sees to his duties.

He hopes that you can forgive him as he is a very busy man and is not in the best health, as you may have heard.

Otherwise, he thanks you for the kind letter and wishes you all the best.

Kind regards,

Keltick.

I began to fold the paper in half, ready to slip it into an envelope and seal it with hot wax. But before I did, I stared at the letter.

Something was missing.

I dipped my quill in ink and began again.

P.S. I thoroughly enjoyed reading your letter, Karness and look forward to hearing from you again, sooner rather than later.

I placed my quill to the side. That would do.

I nodded to myself, before tipping over a minuscule amount of hot crimson-coloured wax onto the envelope's opening. I took out my stamp with the insignia of the crown and crushed it into the wax, waiting until it dried.

I stared at the envelope with my hands on my hips, grinning at my hard work. That is until I remembered the other four hundred or so letters that were still standing on my desk.

But to tell you the truth, I wasn't at all bothered by that reminder. Yes, some of these letters were going to be challenging, requiring replies that made Karness' letter look like nothing more than a sentence.

Because with each envelope I opened, I felt it would bring me just that little bit closer to Karness' next letter.

Seris hadn't looked at me throughout the entire story. He'd been sitting across from me, looking out into the night.

"So, what happened after?" He asked.

"I sent the letter to my scribes, telling them not to open it and to send it wherever Karness' letter had come from."

"They never told you where it came from?" The Sorcerer was surprised.

"No," I shook my head. "They never knew. That letter would have been passed along a dozen times before it reached me. The only detail I ever got was that it came from the east."

A silence lingered with the occasional crack of burning wood between Seris and me.

"And so she wrote back?" Seris asked.

I nodded, "She did. It took the better part of a month, but eventually, her letter came to me, tied up with another set of drawings." I took the letter out of my jacket, trying my best not to crinkle it more than it already was.

Seris finally turned to me, perplexed by the paper I was holding. "You kept it?"

"I kept all of them."

"Why?"

"Because..." I hesitated, searching up at the stars for the answer. "She was the only thing that gave me...purpose, and made me feel like I was no longer alone in that god-forsaken room."

"You weren't alone, sire," Seris uttered. "You had your son. Friends and family. You had the *entire* kingdom."

"Which is why I couldn't talk to anyone," I blurted out far too loudly. "No matter who I went to, I was always seen as the king, first and foremost. Not Deveric, but the king. Do you have any idea what that's like?"

Seris lowered his gaze to the fire. "So that's why you lied to her."

"Excuse me?"

"Karness. That's why you told her you were a scribe. That your name was Keltick. You didn't want her to treat you like a king but as a—."

"I wanted her to treat me like a person!" I snapped, testing my voice's strength. "Sure, I may have had to make up a few stories and details here and there, but our letters were honest and pure."

"And what's going to happen when you find her? Are you going to tell her the truth?"

I opened my mouth to respond but emitted only silence.

"That's what I thought," Seris scoffed.

Dammit, Seris was right. If I did end up finding Karness, the Gods and I knew that I wouldn't be able to tell her the truth. The moment she saw me, the real me, she'd become intimidated, or worse, she'd curse me for lying to her for all these years.

And I didn't want that to be one of the last things to happen to me before I died.

Seris stood up from his seat, exhaling what I imagined was a great deal of frustration. "Do you even know where she is?"

I shook my head. "All I have to find her are her letters." I began to take out every letter from my pack, piling them neatly in my hands. "I could only ever guess where she was.

In a town by the coast that was a short day ride away from the mountains.”

Seris’ eyes darted between the letters and me, flicking back and forth like a swing set. He stretched out his hand and waved it toward him. “Give them here.”

I tightened my grip on the letters, reluctant and aware of the ongoing fire between us. “Why?”

“You want to find her, don’t you?” He asked.

I nodded, still clinging to the letters.

“Then perhaps I’ll be able to pinpoint where she is.”

Every fibre of my body told me not to listen to Seris. That the moment I gave him those letters, he’d cast them into the fire. But at the same time, maybe he was the only hope I had of finding her. Maybe, I wasn’t supposed to figure this out all on my own.

I groaned, lowering my head. “Okay.” I handed him the letters, still feeling the soft material linger on my fingertips.

“Now, I can’t make any promises, but give it time. I’m sure I’ll be able to gather an idea of where she is.”

The sorcerer began to look over the letters as he entered the tent. Before he did, I said, “Seris.”

He paused, glancing at me with no clear emotion. “Thank you. And...I’m sorry I lied to you.”

“It’s okay, my...Deveric.” He smiled, “Thank you,” he looked at the letters. “I know how personal these can be.”

Yes. The letters Karness and I shared were indeed personal. Despite the number of times I lied about who I was, there was still some truth in the things I told her. When Karness told me about her first time trying to fish, I told her how I fell in a pile of manure during my first attempt at horse riding. When she confessed that she was afraid of the dark, I confessed that I was afraid of dogs.

We each shared our lives, one letter after another. We probably knew each other better than we knew ourselves.

And yet, we had never met each other. And we probably never would. Sure, we may find one another in the same room one day, and talk like old friends. But that didn't mean she would ever learn who I *really* was.

If she did, I don't know if she'd ever forgive me.

New Company

Dear Keltick,

Did you know that the first contortionist was a man who escaped prison by hiding in a vase?

A vase? How? Have you seen a vase? They're tiny!

For context, my town was recently visited by a group of performers. They weren't exactly a circus, as they were just passing through, but still, they made the effort to put on a show.

As you can tell, I was both impressed and a bit envious of just how much those contortionists could bend.

If I were that flexible, I'd probably hide in the most discreet places just to scare the living hell out of my father.

He'd probably scold me and threaten to wrap my legs around my head. But I know eventually he'd look back and laugh about it one day.

Honestly, I was amazed by everything I saw today. This had to be one of the most exciting days of my life.

Morning arrived with a sting in my eyes. Light had snuck through the smallest opening of our tent and decided to pick on me. I turned around, grabbed one of my pillows, and blocked the morning sun.

Slowly, I felt sleep pulling me back under.

That is until I heard a voice call out, "Hello there."

The voice was deep and far too dramatic to be considered 'normal.' It was the kind of voice needed to make boring announcements such as 'Don't forget to leave the seat up,' all the more memorable.

I winced as the melodramatic voice continued, becoming softer but not soft enough for my ears to ignore.

"Greetings," Seris said. Judging by the way his words pierced my eardrums, he wasn't far from the tent. I let out an exasperated groan into my pillow, but even that wasn't enough to dampen my frustration.

Please just let me sleep for another hour.

After another minute of Seris and the stranger conversing, I decided through sheer pain that it was time to get up. I finished buttoning up my overshirt and slipped on my coat before stepping outside. The light hit me the moment I exited the tent, nearly blinding me. It was as if the Gods were convinced I was a vampire, aiming the sun directly at me.

I groaned, alive but raising my palm as a makeshift shield. Where was that straw hat when I needed it?

"Ah, you're finally awake," Seris said, unimpressed.

"Thanks to you," I grumbled. "What's going on?"

Seris cleared his throat just as my eyes began to adjust and accept the morning. "Keltick, this is Master Benedict Accard."

Seris' hand was pointed at a short man, or rather a dwarf, no taller than four feet tall. He had a wonderful beard that was dyed a different colour for each braid. His clothes, too, were awfully colourful, making him stand out in a ten-kilometre radius. It didn't help as well that he was standing next to a donkey.

"How do you do?" I asked, forcing a smile.

"I do well," Master Benedict replied matter of factly.

Hmmm. I cocked a brow. Even though I'd uttered only four words, and he'd said only three, I can't say I've ever met someone quite like Master Benedict before. He had an odd energy to him and stood like a crowd of people were always eyeing him.

"We were just discussing you, actually," Seris said to me.

"Oh really?" I asked.

Master Benedict grinned. "Apparently, you've never seen nor attended a circus before. At least that's what this one said." The dwarf pointed at Seris.

A circus?

"That's right..." I darted my eyes between the sorcerer and dwarf, "I haven't."

Where was this going?

As if on cue, a line of wagons, all occupied with other odd and colourful folk, began to move in towards Seris and me. There had to be at least twenty of them, along with two horses to a wagon, all coming from behind the grassy hills around us.

"Well then, you're in luck!" the dwarf bellowed, gesturing towards the wagons. "For tonight, you'll be exposed to the great wonders of Accard!"

Without Master Benedict noticing, I eyed Seris quickly with a look that said, 'Is this guy for real?'

The sorcerer just smiled before nodding.

Damn you, Seris.

"Tonight?" I asked, whilst eyeing the wagons. "Won't it take you a while to, you know...set up?"

"Darn right, you are. Normally, it would take us at least a day or two, depending on how the weather fairs." The dwarf gave Seris a nudge. "But ol' magic man here said he'd be more than happy to help us out. After all, you'd probably want to enjoy yourselves before you head off, right?"

I narrowed my eyes at Seris. How much had he told this dwarf?

"Most indeed," Seris nodded. "However, I'm afraid my time will have to be spent here at our camp, Gods know I have mountains of work to see to. But that won't stop Keltick here from having a fun time."

"Ahh, a shame. But very well." The dwarf clapped his hands together. "How's about we have some breakfast, and then we'll set up the tent. Heaven knows how much easier that'll be with a sorcerer."

A plate was handed to me, holding together some well-done eggs, just as I asked for, with two strips of crispy bacon, a roasted tomato, a piece of toast, and a single sausage. If I had asked for more, they would have had to find me a bigger dish.

Seris and I were underneath the now erect red and white striped tent, standing a total of eighty feet tall and one hundred and twenty feet wide. It was fortunate for Benedict that Seris was able to lift the thing with a simple spell. Without him, they'd have spent hours creating support beams and nailing the tent into the dirt.

"What have you gotten us into, Seris?" I hissed as the Sorcerer sat next to me, his plate only possessing a single piece of buttered toast.

"What?" Seris shrugged. "I thought you'd appreciate this." He looked over at the circus workers' camp.

"We're surrounded by strangers, Seris. What if these people were bandits? Did you think of that?"

Seris bit into his toast. "I faintly remember saying something very similar at the tavern the other night." He hummed.

My face collided with my palm. Goddammit, Seris.

"What's the big idea?" Seris whispered. "Look, we've got ourselves some good food, made by what I can assume to be some good people —or, at the very least, some interesting folk. Isn't that what this was all about? Making some memories before..."

The sorcerer stopped, sighing before taking another bite.

I, too, began to dig into my breakfast, starting with a bite of my bacon, which produced a satisfying crunch.

"We're not wasting time here if that's your concern," Seris insisted. "While you do whatever you wish, I'll hang back and figure out where Karness is."

"You haven't figured it out already?" I asked.

Seris' head fell back a full inch as if shocked. "I'll remind you that you handed me almost ten years' worth of letters, *sir*. You'll be lucky if I can figure out anything."

He had a point there. On average, the response time between letters from Karness and me was somewhere between one and two months. That had to be at least one hundred letters, just from Karness.

I wonder how many trees that would equate to.

"Keltick?" Seris whispered. "You okay?"

"Yeah. I'm just nervous, is all."

Seris nodded, "If you want, we can change our minds and keep heading east. That town you spoke of is only a few—."

"Are you kidding me?" I cut Seris off like he was a wart. "This will be my first circus, Seris!"

No spell could have ever prepared Seris for what I was saying. It was as though all my energy lost throughout my years of being sick had suddenly returned at once. To understand, I have, in fact, never been to a circus or any performance that involved animals, swallowing inanimate objects, breathing fire or having an ungodly amount of hair in the most discrete areas. Of course, I've heard all about these fascinating oddities through the mouths of first-hand witnesses.

"Gods, I hope they have an elephant." I began to frantically look around for any sign of animals.

"Easy, Keltick." Seris tapped me on the arm, making me realise that I was now standing. "There will be plenty of time to see everything. For now, let's just eat and enjoy the morning."

I nodded at Seris' words. Despite how limited my time was, there was still no reason to rush. After all, everything I'd done since leaving Vilton—even something as simple as going out at night for a tinkle—was more exhilarating than ever.

I may have been dying, but I have to say, this was the most I'd ever felt alive.

"You going to stay at camp the whole time?" I asked Seris.

He nodded. "Or until I have the answers."

"That's not fair. You can enjoy yourself too, you know."

"Please," Seris scoffed, setting aside his now empty plate. "I've seen my fair share of circus'. Hell, most of the performances will be nothing compared to what I can do."

"I'll hold you to that."

Seris grinned for a second. Without warning, his eyes shot open as he began to rummage through his cloak. "Where are they?" A few clinks of metal and what I guessed to be a rubber toy squeaked as it bounced in whatever abyss was inside Seris' clothing. "Aha," Seris' voice sang as he pulled out what looked to be two identical gold rings.

"Umm," I stared at him, squinting in confusion. "Usually, you get on one knee for something like this."

Had I not been the king, Seris would have definitely slapped me. However, he sighed and slipped one of the rings on my index finger and the other on his own.

"Stretch out your finger," the sorcerer instructed.

"You better not pull it. I don't know what they put in this sausage." Despite my wittiness, I listened to Seris carefully.

He mirrored my every move and leaned in so that both of our rings were touching.

Seris' voice began to generate a sharp whisper. "In danger, we talk. In darkness, we seek." At that, the two rings began to glow, like a bolt of lightning had struck them and was trapped within. At least for a second.

"What was that?" I turned my hand over, trying to find where the lightning had gone.

"A distress spell." Seris lifted his hand, backside facing me. "Should either of us need to contact the other." He tapped the ring three times with his thumb, creating a bright blue glow. Only the glow came from *my* ring. "Just tap three times, and I'll come find you."

"Huh. Neat." I scanned the ring again, watching as the glow faded after at least half a minute. "Why give this to me now?"

"Well, considering how lacklustre the potions are becoming on you, and the fact that for the first time during this trip, I am leaving you alone, I thought it was very much appropriate."

"Touché," I said.

Seris nodded with a bright smile. "The same will work on yours if you need me. Now," Seris stood up, brushing any crumbs that had fallen on his robes. "If you'll excuse me, I have some letters to read."

Magic, Swords and an Elephant

Dear Karness,

Today I caught myself thinking about you and your last letter. Normally I would take another day or two to write up my response, but I knew this could not wait.

To answer your question, no. I am not a fan of cheese. Nor will I ever be, for that matter. And before you conjure any ideas, just remember, if I suspect you've smuggled a piece of brie or cheddar in your next letter, I'll toss it out the window.

I will have cheese occasionally. But with me, there are some regulations I will always require. I don't like cheese when it's too stringy or stinky. I don't like it when it makes me think I just tipped a bucket of salt on my tongue. Nor do I like it when it's acidic.

Honestly, the only dishes that I would be enthusiastic to have with it would be...bread? I had to think about that for a second. Oh, maybe a pasta dish too, depending on how it's done.

Now, with all this in mind, I don't think I'm that awful. I may not be as fancy or luxurious as you, Karness, when it comes to the cheese community, but be thankful you didn't know my wife.

If you think I'm bad with my preferences, you should have met her. The very word almost made her gag, let alone the slightest smell.

But then again, she never had the biggest appetite.

She passed many years ago now. I don't really talk about her much, but I figured this could be my way of touching on the subject. Although she probably wouldn't appreciate the topic of cheese to begin with.

Oh well.

Now I know you're going to ask so I'll save ourselves the backwards and forwards of waiting for our next round of letters.

We were wedded fairly young, more for the benefit of others than through personal intentions.

Both of our families agreed it was a good match and that it would serve the future well. So like most arranged marriages, we met on our wedding day and made introductions there.

We didn't get along straight away but after some time, we began to open up to each other.

Living in the same house tended to do that.

I'm sorry if you felt that I've kept this from you. Like I said, I don't tend to talk about her much, and I hope you'll understand.

What about you, Karness? Is there some mystery man out there you haven't told me about? Was there a time someone proposed to you, and you had to disappoint him by saying, 'Sorry, I've already got a pen pal.'

I'm kidding. But seriously though, are you married? Have these letters secretly been examined by your husband? And if so, how long before he finds me?

I'm eager to hear your reply and for the time being, I'll imagine you laughing ecstatically at my amazing sense of humour when this reaches you.

From Keltick.

P.S. I'm serious. Don't you dare put a piece of cheese in your next letter.

As the sun descended, the crowds began to grow exponentially. People were swarming the red and white tent from all directions, paying for entry before running off to whatever attraction they preferred.

I stood alongside Master Benedict, who stood with his hands on his hips, admiring the incoming customers.

"'Tis a lovely sight," he said.

"It is," I replied. There were so many families gathering around the tent, with fathers holding their son or daughter atop their shoulders, granting them a better view of the spectacle.

They must have caught a good sight, for their faces lit up like a candle.

I wonder how my son is faring. Does he still grieve my reported passing, or was he already set on being the kingdom's ruler?

I turned my eyes elsewhere.

"Something the matter?" Master Benedict asked.

"No," I muttered. "It's just been a while since I've been home, is all."

"Ahh, yes. I'm with you there." The dwarf sighed. "Twenty years since I left home, now. And not a day goes by that I don't think of it."

"Twenty years?"

"Mhmm. Left when I was just a lad searching for adventure and fortune."

I scanned the field, eyeing all of the workers and circus performers. "And did you find that?"

The dwarf gawked at me, unprepared for that question. I almost began to apologise but he raised his palm to stop me.

"It might not be what I had in mind. Frankly, I would have liked a couple of dragons to fight and a sack of gold to sleep on. But...yes. This is the greatest adventure in the world. And these people make me feel like the richest man alive."

He smiled through his bushy beard, watching as the sun finally began to hide behind the hills. The night was here and so that meant it was almost show time.

"And what about you, Keltick?" Master Benedict asked. "What are you searching for?"

The question was one I had asked myself many times throughout this trip. Of course, my answer went immediately to *her*. But it was more than that. Karness was my destination, but that didn't mean I was to ignore the rest of the journey.

Fishing, drinking, singing, strolling across the countryside with a companion. And now I was about to attend a circus.

"A life worth living."

"And what does that look like to you?"

I squared my shoulders, "Life is about duty. About doing the things that need to be done."

"True, duty is honourable and a necessary thing," the dwarf nodded. "But isn't life also about...ahh how do your people say it? Fun? Excitement? What good is life if there are no times to spend in celebration? Through joy? Whether it be over a meal or a drink."

"But what if duty is all you've know?" I asked.

"Then I pity and envy that man. Whomever he shall be." He gave me a wink. "For he has the chance to finally learn what it is to live. And that's all we can ever hope for."

Despite how soft his words were, I could feel them echo inside me, reminding me over and over again. *Learn what it is to live.*

Master Benedict gave his back a stretch, letting out a long and exaggerated groan. "Guess I ought to head down there. Heavens know the people will want to get their money's worth."

I nodded, watching as Master Benedict began to descend the grassy hill.

"Don't linger too long, sir. You'll miss out on a great show. Oh and make sure to stay for the elephant."

My subconscious took over for me, smiling in response. But then I blinked and realised just what he had said. "Wait? A what?"

Never in my life had I seen an elephant or most of the animals they had here tonight. Monkeys, giraffes, bears, clowns. Oh wait, those were just people in makeup. My bad.

Judging from the way my body was shaking, it was easy to say that I was excited for the sights tonight.

Upon entering, I was recognised by some of the workers for being Seris' companion, and so I was granted free entry. Seris had given me some money on the off chance they would still charge me, so I decided I'd treat myself to a snack instead.

The only thing I could find was this odd, pyramid-shaped squishy thing called 'candy corn' that tasted awfully like honey, butter and vanilla, depending on what coloured part I bit into.

At first, the taste made my face shrink with disgust, but after a couple of handfuls, I began to slowly appreciate it. But where was the corn exactly? In the centre? Or was it at the bottom of the packet? Sweets always had the stupidest names. Why didn't they just call this a 'squishy?' That would have made it all the more appealing.

I entered the main ring of the tent and found myself a seat at the front of the row. The floor was a dark shade of purple and held golden stars patterned randomly along it. In the centre was a single platform, standing at around the height of my hip but was around two metres wide. Lanterns surrounded the ring, lighting it enough so everyone could find their seats and see the show.

A light drumming was coming from behind the tent's curtain, creating a sense of suspense that was slowly building. I sat and waited with my now half-empty bag of candy corn, watching as the crowds shuffled into their positions.

All of the seats were now occupied, making the tent just that little more claustrophobic. But that didn't stop the people from coming in. People were standing at the back, waiting with anticipation.

Gods, how did we never have a circus at Vilton? I asked myself. But that was before I realised that there was a good chance we had, and I was simply too sick to attend.

Bummer.

But here I was, at last, sitting eagerly with my elbows on my knees, leaning forward so that I didn't miss a moment.

The drums ceased, and so did the murmurs of the audience.

This is going to be great.

The curtains, which I suspected were hiding the performers and animals, opened slightly, revealing Master Benedict, now wearing a full buttoned suit of burgundy red, with a top hat as black as the night. Talk about showmanship. With that outfit, you almost forgot about his colourfully braided beard.

He proceeded to the centre of the stage, walking with a cane in hand. He stopped as he reached the centre, eyeing the platform like he was strategising a battle. It was close to the height of his shoulders, almost blocking him entirely from the audience.

A few laughs came here and there, amused by the struggle.

Master Benedict turned to the audience, puzzled. He crossed his arms, tapping his foot in thought. Then he turned back to the curtain and snapped his fingers.

There, without a word of warning, came out a monkey. It bounced around like it were a ball, advancing toward Master Benedict. It held a stool high above its head, holding it like it was prepared for a bar fight.

The crowd and I roared with contagious laughter, not at all expecting such a spectacle.

The monkey dropped the stool in front of the dwarf before being patted on the head. Master Benedict pointed at the curtain, to which the furry helper returned, bouncing with every step.

The ringmaster stood atop the stool and finally set himself in the middle of the stage, posing with his arms above him.

"Welcome, ladies and gentlemen! Boys and girls! Monkeys and people!"

Another wave of laughter blew through the room, showing no sign of dissipating.

"Thank you, and welcome to the great wonders of Accard!" A round of applause began, to which Master Benedict bowed.

Gods, if this was how the crowd was at the start of the show, then I was eager to see them at the end. Benedict Accard would have to be careful; at this rate, he may give a few of the older members of the audience a heart attack.

With me included.

"Tonight," The ringmaster continued. "you will see things that no man has ever seen. Wonders even the Gods themselves would struggle to comprehend. So," he clapped his hands together, "let us start with some magic!"

I smiled, half expecting Seris to jump from the curtain with fire emitting from his hands.

Instead, the audience and I were met by a man dressed in a black suit, with a red scarf wrapped around his neck.

His hair was slicked back with grease, and he had a thick twirly moustache with God knows how many oils within it.

"Tonight, we have ourselves a sorcerer from the great Mountains of Qiwa. Taught by the ten masters of illusion. Ladies and gentlemen, do trust me when I say you do not want to mess with this man. For he can spit—."

At that, the man began to shoot fire from his mouth like he were a dragon, although he aimed at the sky and not at the terrified children that gathered around the barrier.

Or me. My life already had more pyromancers than I could handle.

The fire stopped, and suddenly, the sorcerer began to clench his stomach, appearing to be in an incredible amount of pain. The ringmaster dashed to the sorcerer, patting him on the back before wrapping his arms around the man and squeezing with all his might.

What in the world? A few murmurs of concern sounded around the room.

The sorcerer turned towards me, to which I made a shield with my hands, not at all wanting to be spewed on. But after a great many squeezes, something finally came out of the sorcerer's mouth. Something that moved, and—unlike my experiences—wasn't covered in half-digested carrot.

A rabbit. Not cooked or, god forbid, raw, but a live rabbit, perfectly untouched by whatever else was inside the sorcerer's stomach. The audience and I gasped at that, before clapping as though we had witnessed a miracle.

Seris had never done something like that before, I thought, grateful. If he had, I don't think I could ever look at him or rabbits the same again. *But then again, that's assuming this man was truly a sorcerer.*

The rabbit was as white as snow and looked to have been generously fed. Master Benedict lifted the rabbit before placing it on the floor.

A man beside me gave me a nudge and said, "I hope for his sake that's not where the elephant is."

I chuckled. "Me neither."

After an entourage of jugglers who escalated the risk with each act—starting with simple balls, moving on to lit torches, and ending in swords that seemed ready to slice the world in two—the trapeze acts began.

With no time to spare, Master Benedict and his staff set up the metal straps and rope from the ceiling, hanging them so that they stood close to ten metres from the ground. From there, a group of four or five—my eyes couldn't quite see them—young men and women stood along two platforms, one on each side holding a trapeze bar in hand.

"What are they doing?" I asked the man beside me.

He snickered. "Just you wait and see."

Oh no, I thought, guessing what was about to happen but wincing regardless.

With the drums beginning again and reaching a speed that could go no faster, the man and woman left their platforms, hands grasping the bar with a thick layer of chalk.

The two flew against the air, hands holding firm until they met in the middle. Everyone sat silently, watching as though nothing else mattered. Considering there was no safety net present, it was fair to say that that was the case.

The woman let go of the bar before performing a perfect yet terrifying somersault in the air. My heart almost gave out. Dammit, this show was amazing but it made me feel like a concerned parent.

The woman's flip was completed. After appearing to float for a second, she began to descend before meeting the man in the middle, grabbing his legs with what I hoped was all her strength.

Don't fall. Don't fall.

She stayed attached, gliding with her fellow performer back to the platform.

I sighed with heavy relief as the audience tested my eardrums.

After the act had concluded, which I was thankful for as the same act had occurred but with twice as many people, Master Benedict returned and asked the crowd how everything was so far. Judging by the cheers, it was fair to say that everyone was entertained.

The monkey returned, now holding a hoop, just as a bear charged out and effortlessly jumped through the ring.

Now, I don't mean to sound like a downer, but I had to admit, the show was starting to feel exhausting. Not because I was tired or bored, but because it was one breathtaking spectacle after another.

It hadn't helped that the bear had once again spiked my adrenaline after only just easing from the trapeze act.

After another dozen jumps between the monkey and bear, the animals began to depart.

Thank god, I felt at my chest, checking that my heart had calmed to a normal rate.

"Now," the ringmaster began again.

Dammit.

"We have one last act for the night. But for any who wish to come again, we will be showcasing a dozen of our new acts tomorrow." Master Benedict felt at one of his beard braids before turning towards me, winking.

Was that at me?

"Has anyone here seen...an elephant before?" The ringmaster asked, gazing across the tent with narrow eyes.

I almost jumped out of my seat.

All my life, I'd heard about strange beasts and wildlife across the world. Alligators, goblins, dragons, a Phoenix, a sphinx, and even the unicorn. Of course, some of these had grown extinct, while others were completely foreign to this land. The most interesting animal I'd seen—besides the stool-holding monkey and Mr Lixx, my barber, who had more in common with a cow—was a wolf. Which is just a dog with anger issues and less adorably floppy ears.

But an elephant, that was something different. They were known to only come from one part of the world in the West, and even then, it was hard to bring them overseas via ship. Now that I thought about it, if there truly was a live elephant here, was it legal to own it?

I shook my head. It didn't matter. I was permanently off duty and to be honest, I couldn't care. I just wanted to see the goddamn elephant. Now!

"Behold!" Master Benedict gestured to the curtains that were now completely open.

The ground began to tremble with each shake growing more intense one after the other. I could feel the animal's footsteps rumbling through the ground, up into my very bones. A loud, almost trumpet-like sound came from beyond, causing many, and you better believe myself included, to jump.

"Hey," the man next to me gave me a tap. I remained staring at the open curtains, awaiting the great beast to appear. "Hey. What's with your ring?"

"Huh?" I looked to the man, then to my ring, the one Seris had given me.

It was glowing like lightning was inside it, wanting desperately to get out.

"Oh no," I said. I flicked my eyes to the curtains and then the ring repeatedly. Dammit, dammit.

"Is everything okay? The man asked. But by then I was already up, rushing towards the exit while cursing at Seris.

Damn you, Seris. If I never get to see an elephant, I'm going to pull one out of your stomach.

A Little Rusty

Dear Karness,

You've asked me many times by now, and considering I don't have the physical power to shut you up, I figured it was time I answered your question.

Yes, I have served in the military before. No, I wasn't some general known to have never lost a battle. I wasn't a lone wolf that defeated a hundred men single-handedly.

To be honest, that would be so freaking cool. If that were the case, I would have changed my name to Sir Kicks Ass Alot.

But no. I was neither a general nor a one-man army. Like most men sent to war, I was settled into a division, handed a sword, and sent to fight.

And, of course, I came back, alive and lucky.

I know you'll ask me, so I'll save us the back and forth. You're welcome.

Did I enjoy it? Wow, how forward of you, that's a difficult question to start with.

Yes and no. To me, the war was about much more than just fighting the enemy. It was about saving our people, about completing the mission our King had bestowed upon us.

Did I ever kill anyone? Yes. If I hadn't, I fear I wouldn't have lived to see today. Once again, I didn't want to kill anyone, nor did I ever enjoy it. For me, it was about a higher purpose.

Unfortunately, I knew a fair few who enjoyed the art of violence. Too many times, I saw them take advantage of a siege. Too many times I saw them take advantage of the vulnerable.

I'm glad I never became one of those men.

But to tell you the truth—and there's not many I would share that with—I think my days of fighting finished a long time ago.

I growled as I pushed open the circus tent's flaps, exposing me to the night's cool air. I could hear the crowd gasp as I continued onward, heading back towards camp.

"Bloody stupid, Seris," I kicked a nearby pebble, sending it out towards nothing but darkness.

What could Seris possibly need me for? Had he made some sort of revelation about Karness? No, he wouldn't call me for that. If he'd learnt anything, he would have told me after the show.

The more I thought about it, the more I became concerned. Seris was a cautious man. There had to be a valid reason for signalling me to return. I began to pace myself, accelerating towards the top of the hills.

Gods, there was no conceivable way I could do this without Seris' potion. Without him, I wouldn't be able to crawl, let alone run.

I glanced back towards the circus, watching the shadows pass along the red and white striped tent.

Don't think about it, I told myself. Even without seeing the elephant, the night was still one of pure joy. There was no point lingering on what had been missed out on.

I'd seen some of the world's greatest wonders and for the time being, I had air in my lungs. That was all that I needed.

However, what I could really use now was a glass of chilled water and a massage along my upper back. But that would have to wait. Right now, I needed to get back to Seris. For all I knew, the man had set his hands on fire and had begun to—

"Oh no." In front of me, along a small plain of grass and surrounding oak trees, a fire was building. It festered along our tent and the surrounding greenery, creating an unhealthy competition with the lights of the circus.

"Seris!" I called as I ran down the last hill.

Already, I imagined Seris on the ground, burnt like crispy bacon but without the intoxicating smell.

I heaved with every desperate step. Not because I knew that without Seris, I was as good as dead—well, dead-er, considering I was already teetering on the edge. No, I rushed toward the burning camp because Seris was my friend. He'd done the impossible for me when he could have just left me alone in bed until I passed from this world.

With another minute of running ahead of me, I began to slow. Voices were calling out like brutes into the night. I didn't recognise any of the voices, nor did I consider any of them to be friendly. They were the kind of voices that told you everything about the person, with the way they stretched out their 'e's' and 'a's' and shortened words that already contained only two syllables.

I backed up a step, not at all liking the situation. My eyes scanned the area, now that they were at last adjusted to the night and the fire's glow.

"Where the hell are you, Seris?"

The voices echoed along the field. Who they belonged to, I couldn't answer, but I wasn't at all ready to reveal myself to them. The tent was still burning, rising to around three metres high. My body became prone to the earth, remembering its days in the mud during the war. This was not at all different from those days, but I had to confess I felt nowhere near as confident as I had then.

This body was aged and hadn't touched a sword or lance in over a decade. I would have been better off fleeing or burying myself in the dirt. Now that I think of it, it would certainly make my funeral all the more easier.

Suddenly, I heard footsteps behind me. I immediately spun myself around, ready to kick whoever was trying to sneak up on me.

"Stop," Seris hissed, shaking his hands back and forth.

"Gods," I sighed, "Seris, what's going—."

"Shh," Seris lowered himself to the ground. He appeared to have just come out of the fire, as there was black smeared all along his robes and ash staining his glasses. On closer inspection, I noticed that one of the lenses was cracked too.

"Bandits," Seris gasped as though he'd taken his first breath of fresh air. "They set fire to the tent and tried to capture me."

"What?" I asked, darting towards the tent. "How many?"

"I don't know. Five or six. Maybe. It doesn't matter, we have to go."

"Wait," I said just as Seris began to rise. "Where are the letters?"

Seris' eyes flew away like a frightened bird.

"Seris," I said, with my kingly voice, knowing full well that would get the answer out of him.

"They took them, along with everything else in the tent."

I growled deeply, eyeing the sorcerer. "I thought no one was supposed to know we were here."

"The spell only works while I'm *in* the tent. It won't remain invisible while I go out for a piss."

My head collapsed into the dirt, groaning as quietly as I could.

"It doesn't matter. We don't need them anymore," Seris whispered.

The sorcerer watched as I turned back to him, curious as to what he meant.

"I know where she is. At least, I think I do."

"What?" I leaned closer to Seris. "How sure are you?"

"At least ninety per cent." Seris blinked with watery eyes. How long had he been near the flames?

By now, the tent had collapsed and was reduced to ash. The smell was odd, for it was still smokey but had the occasional hints of herbs, rich spices and...fruit?

"Damn it," Seris cursed. "There goes all of my ingredients."

"They're still nearby," I said, guessing they weren't too far away from the fire. That meant we could find them. And I could get back those letters. "If we surprise them, we'll have a good chance."

"My liege?" Seris returned to his old habits; luckily for him, I wasn't in the mood for slapping. Instead, I wanted to fight. And make these thieves pay. "A good chance at what?"

These bandits held one of the last few things in this world that I loved. Karness' words were what kept me sane.

She was the only one besides Seris or my doctors who kept me company in that godforsaken room. Weeks, sometimes months would go by when it was only me and her letters. They'd excite me upon opening them and would brighten my mood until I read them ten times repeatedly. But afterwards, I would look up from the dried ink, only to find myself alone.

Karness was the only reason I was here today.

I believed Seris when he said he knew where she was. But that didn't mean I was ready to abandon all that we'd ever had. To take her letters was to take her. And I was not about to let these men destroy her beautiful work. Not while I was still breathing.

"Can you conjure me a weapon? A sword or a spear?" I asked, eyes remaining on the burning tent.

Seris nodded, although he wasn't exactly enthusiastic. Perhaps it was because he noticed that my jaw was clenched or because my eyes were reflecting the firelight. Or maybe it was because the thought of fighting these scum had sparked something I thought was put away for good. Sure, this would be nothing like the sacking of Vilton or the one-hundred-day battle of the glacial islands. But by the gods, I was going to fight like it was.

"Good," I said, firmly, not realising my hands were clenched and shaking.

"But sire, we're outnumbered. And I've never fought—."

As if my hands had minds of their own, I snatched Seris by the collar of his robes, pulling him so he could feel my breath. "You're a goddamn sorcerer, Seris. You have the power to shake the world, to emit fire. You can literally shoot lighting from your freaking fingertips." I took in a sharp inhale. "Show them why you shouldn't mess with a sorcerer. Show them...why studying is awesome."

I released my hands from Seris' robe. Luckily, it hadn't torn, although I had some charcoal spread along on my hands. Seris eyed me for a second, digesting every word like it were one of his concoctions. He turned back to what was left of our camp, his face becoming firmer, with a vein beginning to pulp along his forehead.

My heart almost skipped a beat at that. To have Seris argue with me the other day, I was somewhat taken aback. But now, I was deeply disturbed.

But that was what we needed. In a battle, passion and care had to be put aside. In battle, all you needed was your body and some ferocity.

And by all the gods, this young man beside me was full of it.

Seris snapped back to me, a fire alighting within his irises. "Let's go show those bastards who rules this land."

He clicked his fingers, to which a sword appeared out of thin air and floated into my hand.

Oh yeah.

The call to fight was here, at last. For years, I believed I would never again feel the cool touch of a blade and its handle. I thought that the last weapon I would ever hold was a tissue after I had sneezed and regurgitated whatever mucus monstrosity I had brought to life.

By now, I began to descend from my vantage point of the camp, pacing myself carefully alone.

Seris and I agreed that his abilities were better suited at a distance while mine were up close. Although it took some convincing for him to allow me to be put in danger, Seris ultimately agreed.

The fire had dwindled to a smaller, more contained blaze, perfect for putting some meat on a spit roast. As I neared, I finally began to make out the shapes of our thieves.

I squinted as my eyes adjusted, counting five men, all armed and wearing black clothing. One of them, who I guessed to be their leader, was beefier than the others. He had a long ponytail that fell to the middle of his back and wore a plate of armour harnessed around his shoulder.

I tightened my grip along my sword handle. I had to admit, I was curious just how lifelike this conjured blade would act. So far, it felt lighter than it appeared and glowed with a faint glimmer at its hilt.

"Eyes up, gentlemen," the bandit leader said. "We've got company."

"What do we have here?" One of the bandits spoke, eyeing me while he chewed on his fingernails.

"Looks like one of the circus animals got loose," another said. This one was the most *normal-looking* of the group, although his fly was undone and revealed a pair of bright pink undergarments.

The men barked like a clan of hyenas, laughing with no sign of an end.

"What are you doing here?" The group's leader asked, firmly.

"You took my stuff," I said, pointing at them with my sword. "I want it back."

The group all took a moment and looked at each other, waiting for someone to respond. Instead, they just laughed. They laughed and laughed until their lungs were empty and they were left gasping for air.

"You done?" I asked, keeping my eyes fixed on the leader.

The leader scoffed. "You've got guts, man. I'll give you that." He leaned down before lifting what had to be the largest axe I'd ever seen. The thing had to be nearly as tall as me, which, sorry to say, I don't intend on telling. But let's just say the axe was very big and made me begin to regret this idea.

That was until I saw one of the men, standing in the back, scrunching my letters in his hand.

All of the thieves followed their leader, gathering their weapons like a band ready to play.

"You ready?" Their leader asked.

I smiled. "Yeah. Now, Seris!"

Like a star falling from the heavens, a great ball of light sparked from one of the nearby hills. The light blinded the men and myself, almost as though the sun had decided to come home early. I ran back until I felt it was safe, and then suddenly, a great crack sounded in front of me.

I gasped as the sound echoed inside me. Gods, what the hell had Seris just done?

I opened my eyes and, for a second, saw nothing but white light. Fortunately, it passed, although I couldn't exactly say the sight was any better.

The men were dead. All of them had wounds in their chest that singed with smoke.

"Gods," I said to myself. When Seris wanted to be, he was damn effective. I spun to where Seris was standing, lightning still flowing through his hands and fingers. The poor guy was exhausted. His hands were shaking erratically and all the colour in him was drained. Wait, no. Seris wasn't exhausted. His footing was solid and made no sign of collapsing. Why then was he appearing so petrified?

He's afraid. I looked at the dead men again. *Seris had never killed nor even fought—dammit.*

"Seris," I called to him, hoping that my unharmed body would distract him from the sight.

He shook his head, returning to whatever darkness had taken him briefly. "Sire," he said, almost surprised. "I thought I had overdone it."

I scratched my head, trying my best to act natural. "I mean, you could have saved me at least one...but it's okay. You did brilliantly, sir." I gave the man a nod of approval. "Come on down. We can—ahhh."

My body began to tighten at my chest, jolting with uncontrollable pain.

As I fell, I spun my body around so that I faced the dead thieves. No one was behind me. No one alive, that is. So why did it feel like I'd been stabbed? Why was I—

"Seris!" I screamed as the pain spread through my veins, trickling through every fibre of my body. Oh no. It wasn't a knife or an arrow that had struck me. It was another bloody attack. The illness had returned.

So soon?

"Seris!"

My body curled up into a ball, helping bear the pain by just that little bit. It didn't stop me from groaning into the night, but if getting kicked in the privates had taught me anything, this was the best that you could do.

Despite how weary Seris must have been after that spell, the lad still managed to rush down from his spot. "Oh no," the sorcerer kneeled by my side, peering at the remains of our tent. "My potion cache was in the tent when I left."

Oh, you've got to be kidding me.

Seris began to clap at his chest, legs and arms frantically like he was inventing a new dance move. If anyone had walked in at this point, they would have thought he was the one dying and that I was the unfortunate witness.

But finally, Seris stopped before reaching into his robe and pulling out a glass vial.

"Yes. I knew I kept one in there," he said.

Mind you, I was still very much in pain at this point and was waiting fairly patiently on the scorched ground. But had I possessed the ability to speak in comprehensible sentences, I would have said, 'Give me the goddamn potion, you blasting idiot.'

The sorcerer removed the cork with a satisfying pop and lowered it to my mouth. He supported my head as I took the potion, draining it all within two seconds. I gasped. Damn, that was good stuff.

I laid back, wanting nothing more than to fall asleep right here and now. Even if it were next to the dead thieves, my body had no intention of—

"Seris," I said, voice not completely returned.

"Are you okay, sire?"

I pointed at the bodies. "There's only four."

Seris eyed the bandits, his brows furrowing with puzzlement.

And that was when I caught the leader emerging from the night, his axe swinging at Seris.

The weapon collided with the sorcerer, meeting him below the ribs.

No, no, no, no, no, no.

"Seris!" I howled.

The bandit leader retched his axe free from Seris. The sorcerer gasped as he fell limply to the ground.

I shot up from the ground, creating as much distance as I could between the bandit and I.

Dammit, where was my sword? I looked all over the ground, failing to find any sign of it. A cool feeling came at my hand, along with just the slightest amount of weight.

It was the sword. The very same that Seris had conjured. Did that mean he was still alive? I gazed at him as he lay on the ground. Gods, there was already so much blood.

Don't worry, Seris. I'll deal with this bastard.

"You gave me quite a scare there," the bandit said to Seris. He returned to me with an evil gaze, granting me the sight of where Seris' spell had hit him. His face was charred like an overdone steak, sizzling with fresh smoke and an unappetising odour. It didn't help that part of his hair had been caught in the blast.

"You bastard," I said through clenched teeth. "You're gonna pay for that."

"Oh yeah? Well, come here then. I'll have you two re-unite in the afterlife." The man gave his axe a spin, taunting me to draw closer.

But little did he know that I wasn't at all intimidated by him. I didn't care that he had the advantage of having the bigger size and the fact that I hadn't swung a blade in years.

This man had just harmed my friend. And that wasn't something you could *ever* do.

I charged at the man with a war cry I had buried inside me so long ago. The man joined me, although it was obvious that he had had more time to rehearse.

We met in the middle. The bandit swung his axe in a downward strike while I dashed to the right, avoiding it by an embarrassing length. I swung my sword at the man, watching as the blade met nothing but air.

This was strange. My muscles felt as though they couldn't register what I was doing, or why they had returned to their full use. Guess I was going to have to bring them up to speed.

"What was that?" The bandit asked, grinning like a mischievous child. "You call that an attack?" Without hesitating, he flew towards me, this time attempting to prod me with the end of his staff.

I threw myself to the side as if trying to catch a bolt aimed at the king—a move I perfected during my better days on the throne. A poor guard of mine saved me during an attempt on my life at a wedding. One moment, I was cutting the cake and the next, I heard the release of a crossbow bolt colliding with flesh.

Sorry to give you that vivid scene, but I hope it helped you imagine how stupidly and unnecessarily I avoided the man's attack.

My body crashed into the dirt. Had I been just a touch less careful, I probably would have landed on my sword. I tossed and turned before spinning myself around and rising to my feet.

"Have you ever done this before?" The bandit asked, leaning on his axe like he had all the time in the world.

"With all due respect, I've been crossing blades with men since before you were able to wipe your ass." I grinned.

Rather than diminish the man's morale, I instead made him very, very mad. Like, 'I'm about to murder you for fun,' kind of mad.

He charged at me with his axe held high, screaming like a wild animal.

"Don't move until you have your chance," I whispered to myself. He came in closer and closer, readying himself like a battering ram at a city's gate. It would only take another second until he—

I ducked and rolled between the bandit's legs as he closed the distance finally. He groaned as he turned around to see me with my sword stuck in his back, buried until there was nothing else to push through.

He collapsed to his knees, and then finally his face, groaning with one last breath.

I gasped, staring at the enemy I'd downed. "I've still got it."

Departure

My body felt like lead, ready to collapse to the ground. Why was everything so blurry? That only happened after a blow to the head—or when I was dared to spin in circles a dozen times and then try to walk a straight line.

Gods, I really was getting old.

"Seris?" I called out, forgetting where I was in the world. Fighting always had that effect on me.

"Sire..." the sorcerer said faintly. Far too faintly.

The sound of his voice brought a slight glimmer of energy to me. Rest would have to wait until this one was safe and recovered.

I rushed to Seris as fast as I could. He was only lying down a few metres from where I'd killed the bandit, but every second felt vital.

"I'm here, Seris." I knelt beside him, instinctively placing my hand on his wound. Gods, he was bleeding so much. I took the sleeve of my undershirt into my mouth and tore at it until I had a somewhat acceptable bandage. I tied it around the side of Seris, ignoring him as he winced with pain.

"Seris," I tightened the improvised bandage. "What do I do? Is there something in your robe that I—?"

"Shh," Seris whispered. He waved at me to come nearer, as if he only had a dozen words left to speak. "She's in Deston."

"What?"

"Karness. She's in Deston. You're not far, Deveric." The sorcerer's eyes began to flicker slightly, struggling to remain open.

A part of me had completely forgotten about her. The moment I saw the thieves, everything had faded like the wind.

Deston, I thought, vaguely remembering where the town was located. *I really am not far from her.*

"I don't have any more potions," Seris said. "You...you won't have much...time...left. Don't waste this...my king."

I shook my head at his words. "Forget about me for a second, Seris. We've got to get you out of here and find...Seris?"

My eyes fell onto his. They were still open, but they were no longer moving. I shook his body gently. Then again again and again, more firmly after hearing no response.

Before I could speak, a bright glow of blue luminescence came from my hands. I gasped, reacting as though a tarantula had fallen on me. But then, as the glow evaporated, I looked back at my hands. They were different. No longer did they appear like those of a warrior, strong and as tough as steel. They were more than capable of day-to-day functions, but still, it was clear what was happening.

Gods, my breath caught in my chest. *My body*—the disguise was gone. I was myself again.

"Seris!" I shouted. "Seris! Wake up! Don't leave me, dammit."

No matter how much I shook his body, Seris never woke up.

I don't know how long I sat there with Seris in my arms. The more I thought about it, the more it made me want to stay. It would have been easier to just remain there, holding my friend while I waited for my life to consume me.

But that's not what he would have wanted. Seris had gifted me with the most precious thing in the world.

Time.

Despite having at best a single day until my illness finally claimed me, I knew I couldn't leave Seris where he was. The man was a sorcerer. A scholar. A man of honour. And most importantly, a friend. One I damn well didn't deserve.

I used the bandit axe to dig Seris' grave. It was difficult and, at times, downright bloody useless. But I knew this was something I had to do. Something that couldn't be ignored.

If I hadn't done this, I knew I would die with one last regret in mind.

I placed Seris' body down into the grave. I made sure to cover him with his robe out of respect and to leave his glasses on. Gods know he'd need them in the next life. Wherever that may be.

After returning the dirt to the spot, I stood before it with my hands together, almost like I was about to say a prayer. And yet, when it came time to speak, I couldn't find any words.

"I..." each syllable made me tremble. Even though I was familiar with death, the feeling always felt so strange. And so awful. My eyes gazed at the fields, watching as the morning wind blew against the fresh grass and the occasional dandelion.

What would Karness say? I asked myself. She was always the person who knew what to say. Or to write.

At that thought, I turned back towards the thieves, lying dead at the remains of my camp. I eyed the one in the back, realising something that only grief could make me forget.

That man still had my letters in his pocket.

I flattened a piece of parchment carefully before clearing my throat. If I was going to read this out loud, I ought to sound somewhat intelligible. Although it hadn't helped that my original, more growly voice box had returned just hours before.

Oh well. Here it goes.

"'*Dear Keltick.*'" I began reading. "'*I don't know why, but today I wanted to tell you about the happiest day of my life.*

I smiled with quivering lips. I always enjoyed reread-ing this one.

"'My day began when I woke up to a fresh cup of tea, made and delivered to me by my Dad. From there, we had a light but satisfying breakfast that consisted of porridge with some picked berries. So far, this was just like any other day. But for some reason, the day just felt...better, like the sun was just a shade brighter and the air was that little bit fresher. I went for a walk afterwards, leaving Dad to stay home and see to some chores. I asked if he wanted to go, but he knows how much I enjoy my lonesome walks. I always found them intriguing, the way your legs would just take you wherever you wanted to go and find somewhere you'd never been. Plus, I found that it gave me time to think. About life, about the world. About anything.'"

By now, I could feel a trickle fall down my cheek, tickling my flesh with sorrow.

"'I must have walked for half the day then. Normally, I'd call it after an hour and return home, but today, I just wanted to continue on. I wanted to see whatever it was the world had to offer. Whether it be a new face, a dish being served to a young couple or even a group of children playing a ball game. The wonders of life start both so small, and yet they ripple into something grand. I don't know where I'm going with this, but I hope it gives you an idea about life. Perhaps it'll help you realise that it's the little things in this world that stand out the most. You, in all respects, are a

small part of my life. We write to each other when we can or when the post service decides to not be delayed. And yet, we have stuck together throughout that time.'"

I sighed, gazing at the final passage, trying to find the strength to speak the rest. Come on Deveric, you've got this. *"'Everything that happened that day was nothing special, not really. The thing that stuck out was that it was the day your first letter arrived at my house. And I...I have always been grateful for that. For you. For everything. And everyone.'"*

I folded the letter with trembling hands before tucking it with the others in my coat pocket.

My body shook profusely as I took in a deep breath. "I don't know if that was the right thing to say, but..." I kneeled before Seris' grave, placing my palm on the dirt as I closed my eyes. "Farewell, my friend. And thank you. I'll tell Karness you said hello."

The Way

Those several thousand steps I took were the hardest ones in my life.

My body had returned, as well as its lack of physicality. I was still able to take one step after the other, but Gods, Seris' magic was something else. Together, we'd be able to make this final hike before sundown. But now, I didn't know when I would get to Deston. Or if I would.

As I pushed myself forward, a question lingered in my mind: How was I supposed to find Karness' exact location?

And then I asked myself the next question, the very same one that I'd thought about for this entire trip. What was I going to tell her?

"Hi, my name's Keltick. Well, actually it's Deveric. Yes, *that* Deveric. Care to talk quickly before my life slithers away?"

I kicked a stone as I walked along the road due east, trying not to look back towards where I'd left Seris.

I was journeying through the endless fields Seris and I had crossed before running into the circus and Master Benedict. By now, a road stretched ahead, leading to a patch of oak trees. Along it, there was a stream that glided along these dark stones that were layered with moss. The sound of water trickling downstream brought peace to my mind. But even then, it reminded me of Seris, and how much I missed him already.

If I had time, my friend, I'd have buried you atop a mountain with a grave full of books and glass vials. And your favourite hat.

The image of Seris wearing that very hat as we fished made me smile for a second. It was odd how quickly one could be reminded of pain. Just as you thought you were beginning to feel better and forget whatever it was you were sad about, it would always creep back.

But then again, that was the beauty of pain. Remembering.

And remembering why it was painful to begin with.

I sighed, hoping that Deston was close by. It had been a while since I'd studied the towns and villas of my kingdom. Well, study wouldn't be the best word to describe that. In all honestly, it was more like goggling than anything. The map of my kingdom would lay stretched out in front of me, and I would take notes of all the drawings of fields, houses, farms, mines and anything that was considered a landscape.

Geography was never my strong suit, not unless it involved some form of battle tactics. But regardless, I knew in my heart that I had to continue straight. East would bring me Karness, eventually. That or I would collapse and join Seris sooner than I thought.

To pass the time, and avoid thinking about when my next attack would occur, I shuffled through some of Karness' letters, hoping it would give me an idea of what to say when I saw her. Or where she may live in the town. Unfortunately, she never wrote anything that made her house stand out, such as having a red front door or a sign that said, 'Karness lives here. For anyone wanting to meet her, please make an appointment.'

If only that were the case, perhaps then I would have a chance. Perhaps the only way I would be able to locate her would be to ask around and hope no one recognised me. Not that it was likely—people I'd known all my life would fail to recognise me today.

Walking through the markets always brought home the smell of fish. I suppose that's on me for taking a detour when I got bored of my usual route.

I skimmed through the letter, starting another one at random.

The waves have been crashing harder against the docks this winter. I hope nothing bad comes of it. Everyone knows we rely on those for our deliveries from Vilton.

I scanned the parchment thoroughly, trying to find something, anything that may help my search.

Dear Keltick, you should see the mountains here one day.

Dear Keltick, my favourite bar just introduced a new drink, the rib cracker. Wish me luck.

Dear Keltick—

Dear Keltick—

I flicked the pages one after the other, reading the same two words over and over again. I was almost tempted to toss the papers away. Instead, I gripped them harder than I had ever before.

So many lies, I thought. Each of these letters, as well as my own, were lies. And yet they had made my life just that little less miserable. How was she supposed to understand that?

If I tell her, would she smile and say, 'I knew all along,' before curtseying? Or would she threaten me with a butcher's knife before tearing our letters like blades of grass?

Karness didn't deserve to be lied to. Even I had to admit that. She was the most gentle soul I'd ever encountered, even if it were only through words on paper. She shouldn't be disappointed. From the moment I read her first letter, I felt that I knew who she was. And that had only helped as we continued to write to each other through the years.

That's why when I finally found her, I knew she would never forgive me.

A town I'd never seen stood in front of me. It laid across the coast with a dozen or so docks standing with tied ships. I could taste the fresh sea salt air in my lungs. How many years had it been since I'd seen the ocean?

A lifetime ago, I thought.

The temptation to drop to the ground and rest was as tempting as another mug of ale before bed. But on this occasion, my mind had gotten the better of me and was ordering me to get off my ass.

This had to have been Deston. It had to be.

So, like the previous hours I'd spent walking with one hope in mind, I stepped forward.

The signpost at the entrance read 'Deston' along its surface.

"Ahh," I sighed, feeling like I'd dropped a bag of bricks. Let's just hope this wasn't a hallucination and that I wasn't really passed out somewhere on the road. I don't think I'd be able to endure any more disasters throughout the rest of this trip.

Deston, at first and second, all the way to the tenth glance, was nothing special upon entering. It was the typical environment with too many houses in such a minuscule and confined space.

Then again, that was exactly what it was like in the more common parts of Vilton. But that was a city. That was *the* city. Places like that were supposed to be built to contain a large population, but here, it felt off—like the people were gathered for some deeper, driving motive.

Now that I thought about it, maybe it was because of Karness' letters that I pictured this place to be so different. The way she described the people, she made the place feel like a fantasy. Or maybe I was just so used to...what was I used to? A bed to myself with servants to see to my limited needs?

But as I passed through several intersecting streets, I did find something that Karness hadn't exaggerated in her letters. If anything, she hadn't given it proper justice.

The smell of fish lingered like a lost sock in the laundry. No matter where I stood, the scent followed me around.

It made sense for the amount of fish here. Being that the town was by the coast, there would be a decent amount of work to go around for everyone. From sailors to fishermen, marketeers, cooks, and equipment providers. It would've been no surprise if I were to learn that everyone in Deston worked to some extent with the market.

After all, fish was known for being traded and shipped all across the world...just to end up in some arrogant king's mouth.

Ahem.

I crossed one of the market's stalls, eyeing a bass that was stretched across the table.

"Quite a catch," I said to the shopkeeper.

The woman gazed at me with a crooked eye, like I'd just spoken another language. I began to move on but paused and inquired the shopkeeper. "You wouldn't happen to know a woman named Karness, would you?"

She squinted hard this time, making the fish seem all the more attractive.

I sighed, walking towards the closest acceptably pleasant person, which, judging from the crowd so far, was a hell of a way away.

"You'll want to head towards the bay," The shopkeeper said with a croaky voice. "Now, are you going to buy some fish, or are you going to drive the customers away?"

"Huh..." I took a second to register what she had said. "Oh, thank you. Sorry."

She waved her hand at me like she was shooing a feral cat. At that, I aimed myself towards the bay, finding just the smallest gap between the tight streets. The sea was calm today, and yet it could still be heard between the ongoing calls for prices and items for sale.

I'm almost there.

For a small town, everything felt spread out. It was like there were only three commercial properties, each given a third of the town to share. But at the same time, there was a beauty to the place.

Everyone felt connected and familiar with each other. Which was probably why a few people were staring at me as I went past a few alleys that were a little too tight for my comfort.

"Hey, old man," a young voice called to me.

"Old man?" I whispered, taken aback. "I'll have you know I'm forty." I turned to what I expected to be a young brat who was just trying to intimidate me. Instead, it was a group of adolescent brats who did, in fact, intimidate me.

"Whatever, you're not young, so that makes you old."

I mean, he does have a point there. It's terrible logic, but he's not wrong.

"Whatever," I said, shrugging.

"We don't take too kindly with strangers. Not unless you pay a little 'entrance fee.'"

"Entrance fee?" I asked.

"Mhmm," the brat said, holding what looked to be a cudgel. "Ten gold." He stuck his hand out and closed it repeatedly.

"I don't have an ounce of gold on me," I confessed, showing my empty pockets except for the one containing the letters. "My sorcerer was the one with all the gold, I'm afraid. Which makes no sense considering I *am* a king."

The young folks' heads all leaned to the side, trying to comprehend what I'd just said. They all peered at each other, before laughing like I was a circus monkey.

After an unhealthy amount of knee slaps, the young bunch began to step toward me.

"Crud," I whispered before darting away. There was very little hope that I could outrun them, being that the group was all young and frankly more fit than I ever was at that age. Additionally, my legs were not up for the task. They were drained and ached with each second I stood.

"Get him!" One of the juveniles called out, squeaking as his voice made a crack.

I made turns in random directions whenever I could, heading left at the end of the alley before making another down an intersection. Then another and another. I had no idea where I was, and I could feel my body's last ounce of energy withering away.

I didn't believe the kids would do enough harm to kill me, but then again, if I was beaten to a pulp and forced to lie incapacitated, who knew how long it would be before I could attempt to find Karness again?

Or worse, who knew how long it would be before the illness finally took me? For all I knew, I had another hour before an attack came. Hopefully, that wouldn't be the case, as I would very much hate to time it so Karness would see me perish just moments after meeting. Or worse, if I was truly psychotic, I'd time it so I suffered an attack right after she made me a cup of tea.

No. I couldn't do that. To Seris, maybe. But that chance had been missed.

The chasing brats began to quieten from behind, leaving nothing but echoes.

I gasped, falling to the ground, no longer caring if they caught up to me. I needed to rest, at least for a minute. Or an hour. Gods know these legs deserve a rest.

Before long, I got up, dusting any dirt on my trousers before noticing what was in front of me.

The bay.

Platforms of dark decking stood several metres above the shoreline, stretching to where the water began to deepen so that the ships could dock. Along it were these sharp rocks, creating a barrier along crashing waves.

Despite never witnessing this spot, I felt immediately like I'd been here before.

In a way, I had. From the number of letters Karness wrote about the sea, the waves, and the seagulls gliding above the water, I felt that I had pictured this scene many times. All that was missing now was Karness and her boat, sailing out to catch a fine trout.

"There he is," the same squeaky voice called out to me, close enough that I could hear his breath.

Before I could turn around, I felt a large round object collide with my back, causing me to fall to my knees and curdle into a protective ball.

"Get him!" The juveniles chanted together.

"Check his pockets. He's got to have something in them."

I felt hands rummaging at my sides, searching for anything of value. I whimpered as they found nothing and kicked in response. These kids weren't going to find anything they wanted. The only thing I had on me was Karness'—

"What have we got here?" One of the brats pulled out the letters in my coat pocket, snatching them like they were a pack of sweets.

Oh no.

"Letters?" Another spoke. "Who carries letters? Where's the gold, old man?"

A kick connected with my ribs, causing the air in me to escape in a painful grunt.

"Leave him. He's not worth the trouble," one of them said.

The juveniles refrained from harming me any further. I could just faintly hear them walk away, but that was just before I heard a loud and terrible rip. Like lightning that had struck down a tree.

I darted towards the sound, feeling my heart sink like a stone.

"No," I whispered.

All of the letters had been shredded to bits, with half of the pile dipped inside a small puddle, weathering away.

"Karness," I reached out towards the letters. They weren't going anywhere, and yet I felt an unavoidable urge to get to them as soon as possible. But my body would not listen. Everything inside me told me to rest and allow the inevitable to happen.

As I lay on my back, I realised that tears had begun to flood my eyes. I stared at the sky as dark clouds rolled in, bringing forth the rain.

The waves crashed in a perfect sequence of ten seconds, putting me in an almost meditative state.

This would be a nice place to die. I confessed despite my grief. Not many people got to choose where the end happened for them. Some were lucky enough to pass in their sleep or with a loved one or while doing something they loved.

For me, I just wanted to stare up at the sky and watch the world as it became nothing but light.

"Sir?" A voice, thankfully not belonging to the young brats, called out. Normally, I would have jumped at the sudden call, but considering how tired I was, my mind no longer cared for any threat.

"Sir, are you okay?" The voice was gentle and smooth like paper, incapable of creating insult or offence.

My only response was a moan, the kind that was made when your parents told you to wake up at the crack of dawn.

"You poor thing," the voice neared, sounding all the more tender. Maybe I was already dead, and this person was my guide to the next life. But then again, if that were the case, why was I still in so much pain?

My body tingled as the person leaned down and grabbed me by my arm, trying with all their might to lift me.

Dammit, I realised. I wasn't yet dead. There was still some time left for me, after all.

I tried as best I could to raise myself from the damp ground. My body screamed at me, telling me to stop at once.

I still have time, I said to it. *Let me use it before it's too late.*

I rose. Whoever was with me had a firm grip on my side and threw my arm over their shoulders so that I wouldn't lose balance.

"Thank you," I managed to say. My voice had returned to what I'd been used to for so many years. Croaking with a disturbing amount of disease. I hope it didn't turn the person off. I'd very much hate it if they decided that I was better off being left behind.

But luckily, the person held on and slowly but effortfully walked me towards a small house standing in front of the ocean.

At Last

Dear Karness,

I'm sorry.

My eyes had fallen into a deep slumber by the time we reached the house. Judging from how comfortable I felt as I woke, I'd been placed in a bed. And judging from the floral smell in the air, someone was making tea.

I felt my ribs as I got out of bed, mesmerised by how little pain there was, not only where I'd been hit but in my legs as well. I guess all that I needed was a good rest and no one trying to kill me.

The room was fairly spacious, from what I could tell. Not as large as my chambers, of course, but it was safe to assume it was bigger than most bedrooms in this town.

The floors gave off a gentle creak as I left the room, proceeding to an open kitchen that had a pot of boiling water next to a couple of cups holding what I guessed to be dried flowers. I inhaled the fresh smell. Gods, why was it so good?

"You're awake," the stranger said, coming from around the kitchen corner. "I was afraid I was going to drink alone."

I stood there silently, with my heart skipping a beat. I would have thanked her but needed a minute to absorb the view in front of me.

For starters, the stranger was a woman. At least thirty, with straight hair as dark as obsidian and a face that glowed as if enchanted with a spell. Her cheekbones stood atop the corner of her lips and were as sharp as fresh daggers.

She was smiling, which didn't help in encouraging me to respond. Instead of waiting, she gestured to a seat in front of one of the tea cups.

I sat down and watched as she poured the boiling water into my cup, then her own.

"How are you feeling?" She asked.

I cleared my throat, knowing full well it would sound like death had I not. "Better, thank you."

The room was toasty with a lit fire at our sides, granting me a warmth that rivalled her company.

"You gave me quite the scare. I saw you from across my porch and thought you'd been washed up from the shore."

I let out a short laugh, "I would have preferred that."

She paused, before smiling and stirring her tea.

The silence was long and stretched out like an open field. Not to say that that was wrong or awkward, I'm just saying that that was simply what it was and what it needed to be.

"I haven't seen you before," the woman said before blowing on her tea. "Did you just arrive in town?"

"I did," I copied her as she blew and began to take sips. "Gods," I leaned back as the tea coursed down my throat.

"Is everything okay?"

I nodded, taking another sip and sighing. "This has to be the best tea I've ever had."

The woman chuckled, "It never disappoints."

Another silence fell. This one felt more comfortable.

"You were saying?" The woman's eyes flicked towards me.

"I was?" I said, forgetting what we were talking about.

She chuckled for a healthy amount of time, to the point that she had to cover her mouth with her palm. "Sorry. You just remind me of someone."

"Oh? Is he dashingly handsome and has a terrible sense of humour?"

"A terrible sense of humour? Absolutely. Handsome? I wouldn't know." She paused, turning towards a window that faced the ocean. The day had grown darker since I'd fallen, and the rain had only become more torrential.

"You a sailor?" She asked, still staring out into the water.

"No. I'm just a man on a journey." I took another sip of tea, regretting it immediately, for it brought me that little bit closer to the bottom.

The woman granted me the sight of her profile once again, although her brightness had dimmed just a touch.

"And what journey is that?"

"I'm looking for someone."

"Someone?" The woman stopped mid-sip.

"A woman."

"Oh," she made a brazen face with a cocked eyebrow. "You didn't take me for a romantic."

"I didn't say..." It was probably best not to elaborate any further. Denying it would only reveal the truth to her.

"Does she have a name? Maybe I know her."

"She does," I thought of the letters I'd lost, of how their remains were probably blown away by the wind or drenched from the rain.

"Well," the woman waited, smiling with eagerness.

"Karness."

At that, the woman's face dropped like a stone at the top of a mountain. She placed her mug down, calm and controlled.

"What do you want with Karness?" She asked.

"I..." the words were stuck in my throat. Adrenaline began to fuel all my senses. "I have a letter for her."

What had been dark for a moment now shone brighter than ever. The woman's eyes sparked like fiery pyres, and her lips curled into an almost contagious smile.

"Is it from Vilton?" She asked, giddy with excitement.

"Vilton?" I asked, watching as her composure was replaced with an energy I'd never seen.

"I..."

Oh. Oh, you idiot. You stupid, stinking, sick, idiot. You king of fools and manure. Ruler of the dum kingdom.

"You must be Karness," I said. The words felt strange on my tongue, like a wine that had aged for a thousand years.

She nodded dangerously fast. "I am. Oh thank you, thank you, sir. May I have the letter?"

Gods. The knowledge that this woman was *her*. The one I'd spoken to for years, the one with whom I'd shared so much of my life... and she'd shared hers with mine. It made her all the more beautiful. And yet I didn't want to see that smile be stripped away.

"I...I'm afraid I lost it during my travels here."

Karness' face collapsed. It was clear that this was going to hurt her far more than it would ever hurt me.

"Oh," she said, containing her disappointment.

"But," I said, "he did instruct me to remember it, in the case that it was...misplaced."

Her eyes returned to me at once, hopeful. She leaned back in her seat, granting me her full attention. She nodded, as if to say, 'go on.'

I cleared my throat again.

"To Karness. Firstly, I fear I have to apologise for how long it has taken me to write this letter. Every day the words flee from me like a dying breath and I grow more and more frustrated that I cannot simply speak with you as if you were here now. To answer your question, yes, I am doing well; however, If you were here with me now, you'd probably disagree. In all honestly I feel that I am growing tired of this phenomenon called life. Don't worry I am not thinking of that, I am merely growing weary of what I am doing with it. In truth, I have never been satisfied with my life. I look back at all that's passed and think nothing of it. So many days wasted. So many times I wish I was elsewhere. So many days I wish I could be standing with you, telling you everything on my mind. I'm rambling I know, but then again you knew what you were signing up for when we began this journey."

I stopped for a second, looking at Karness to make sure she was still paying attention. Little did I know she had had her eyes closed the entire time, picturing whoever she imagined Keltick to be.

"Keep going," she said.

"To think how many years it's been since we first wrote to one another. I remember thinking you'd never respond. But you did. And to this day I've never regretted one word I've written to you."

I paused again, forgetting what I'd written before I'd left for this journey across the realm. Gods, it had felt like a lifetime ago. So much had happened in so little time, and yet here I was, never wanting it to end.

"Is there any more?" Karness asked.

I shook my head. "That's it."

Karness didn't seem either disappointed or satisfied. Anyone could tell that she appreciated hearing the letter, but as to what it meant, she seemed perplexed. A single tear was rolling down her cheek, to which she immediately wiped it away.

"Sorry," Karness sniffed. "Thank you. I really appreciate you doing that for me."

I nodded. "My pleasure."

The rain dampened the silence then, as did the cracking of wood in her fireplace.

"I suppose you'd want to get going now," Karness sighed. "The post service can be a demanding job, I hear."

"Actually," I lifted my cup, surprised as to how quickly I'd drunk it. "If it wouldn't trouble you. I'd very much like another cup of tea."

Karness smiled at me, and so I returned one to her, hoping it was comforting.

"Of course," she said, before taking my now empty cup and preparing a new one.

"What's he like?" I asked, watching Karness put a fresh pot of water above her fire.

"Who?"

"Keltick," I said.

"Oh," her voice fell again. "He's...he's probably the greatest man I've never met." She faced me, smiling with pain.

"I see."

She reached for a jar of dried flowers and took out a pinch before placing them into a pair of cups.

"He talked about you a lot," I blurted out.

"He did?" Karness asked, her head tilted.

I nodded. "Before I left, he told me all about you. How you wrote to each other, how you'd never met. He said he always wanted to come meet you." I almost confessed right then and there. Inside, my heart wanted to say, 'I'm Keltick!'

Instead, I just continued and watched as the woman's smile in front of me became brighter than the sun. "He also said that he always regretted not being able to say 'thank you.'"

"For what?"

I shrugged, "For keeping him company. For giving him something to look forward to. I don't know. But trust me, dear, when I say I can tell when a man is lying." I shook my head slowly. "And Keltick was no liar. If he could, he'd march through hellfire if it meant he could have one day with you."

Karness stood there quietly, her back facing me as she finished preparing the tea.

"You really mean that?" She asked.

"I do."

Her shoulders began to slump up and down repeatedly. She sniffed, and although she tried to contain it, she was unable to contain her tears for long.

"Gods," she exclaimed, bringing her hands to her eyes.

"Hey, hey, hey," I stood up and moved to her. "It's okay, dear."

"No. It's not. It's not fair. Why do I not get to have what I want? Why do others get to live the lives they dream of?"

I padded my hand on her shoulder, gently pulling her to face me. She followed without protest. And as her reddened eyes met mine, I moved forward, taking my hands and wrapping them around her. She did not resist, and so I held her for as long as she needed.

I took my hand to the back of her head, holding it so she could rest, and let me carry her burden.

"It's okay," I whispered. "It's okay, Karness."

"Why? Why does it hurt so much?"

I rubbed her back gently, and let her lay on my chest. "Because it's true. You two have something that most people dream of finding. Don't let it ache you, dear. Embrace it."

She looked up at me with her reddened eyes, tears falling like the outside rain. "Who are you, really?" She asked.

My heart dropped, struggling to find the right words. "I'm just a man who didn't want to disappoint you."

She stared at me, mouth opening like she was about to speak. Instead, she stepped away, removing herself from my arms. She wiped away her tears and returned to the cups.

Suddenly, an uncomfortable but not painful jolt rose within me, tingling my limbs before spreading within the rest of my body.

No. Not now. Please not now.

I contained a gasp. The last thing I needed was for Karness to see me die. "I'm afraid I may have to pass on the tea," I said, teeth gritting.

"Oh," she sniffed. "That's okay. I guess you'll just have to come by another time Mr...oh. I'm sorry, I don't think I caught your name."

I began to head towards the front door, Karness following me as I did. I opened it, glad that the rain was appearing to subside, as were the clouds above. Perhaps this last day of mine would be worth the trouble.

I laughed, "No, I don't think you did." I offered my hand. "Deveric"

She eyed my hand before taking it into her own, giving it a gentle shake. "It was very nice to meet you, Deveric. Thank you for coming."

"And thank you for saving me."

More than once, I thought.

"Hmm, Deveric," Karness smiled. Gods, how could something as simple as that cause such euphoria? "That's a nice name. I feel like I've heard it before."

I smiled, pleased to see that her mood was slowly returning to its bubbly, normal self.

She'll be alright, I thought. Regardless of how she'd wept now and would most likely weep later, she would manage to move on. Eventually.

I took one last look at Karness, committing every detail to memory—the curve of her smile, the warmth in her eyes, the delicate flutter of her lashes, the shape of her ears, and the texture of her hair. I was confident that this was the most beautiful sight I'd ever witnessed.

I took a step outside and said before leaving her forever, "It's a king's name."

Destination

The sun had come out and decided to rest on my shoulder as I left Karness' house. It warmed me as I journeyed in no particular direction, feeling the incoming doom.

I'd felt some level of closure when I stepped out of her home. She'd learn how I felt about her, and how I wished to thank her for everything she did for me. Of course, there was so much more I wish I could do with my time. Everyone who was close to their end would agree with me on that.

Still, a part of me wished things were different. I wished that I still had years left to live and could spend that time with Karness, drinking tea, and taking her boat out to fish before talking until the sun went down.

In another life, that may happen. But for now, everything was set in stone. Karness would go on with her life and, hopefully, one day, find someone to treat her better than I ever could.

And I would be gone.

I knew the end was close at hand. The more I trudged, the more I was sure that my time was coming close.

Good, I thought. Everything I'd set out to do had been accomplished. And at last, I would be able to rest.

I'd left Deston soon enough, grateful that I hadn't reencountered those brats. I very much would have hated to die from my heart exploding during another chase.

The wind had picked up, and still, the sun continued shining against my body. I became uncomfortably sweaty and so I took off my coat and left it for whoever wished to claim it.

I walked and walked across the green fields once again, seeing no end nor any beginning in them. If I could, I'd walk these hills forever, holding Karness' hand with mine. We would talk about anything we wanted and let the world witness our endless banter.

I smiled at the thought. That *would* be nice.

As I crossed yet another hill, I began to feel my legs shiver. Poor things, they'd done nothing but transport me across the country.

"Don't worry, guys," I squeezed my thighs. "We're almost there."

There stood another hill in front of me; only this one held a single tree at its top. By now, I was practically dripping with sweat and wouldn't mind some shade. I climbed the hill with great effort, using my hands and feet to make the last couple of steps. Letting out a much-needed sigh, I turned back to see all that I'd conquered.

I let out a loud "Woo!" It echoed into nothingness, allowing only the world and I to enjoy it.

From here, I could just barely make out Deston. The town was almost as insignificant as an ant.

But little did everyone know that there was a woman in that town, a gorgeous woman who could make even an undertaker smile. She had changed not just my life but the life of a king.

And she had kept me alive for so long.

A great wave of clarity washed over me atop that hill. I was thankful that I had made it to say 'thank you,' to Karness.

I wandered towards the lonesome tree. It stood majestically towards the sky with branches spread like open arms, inviting me to come closer. The shade it granted me was so stimulating that I sighed, thankful for its protection.

My body began to jolt again, still not painful but only slightly discomforting. I sat down and leaned against the tree's body, surprised by how well it suited my back.

"I think I'll just rest here for a while." I closed my eyes for a second, inhaling the fresh air.

Another jolt came, spreading to all points of my body.

I held onto my breath like I was holding Karness.

Suddenly, I felt sparks alight behind my eyes. Everything and everyone I'd ever encountered was in front of me now. My son. My wife. Friends and family I'd thought I'd forgotten. Seris cooking the fish we'd caught together. The men and women I'd sung and drank with. Master Benedict and his wonderful show.

And then, finally, Karness, who smiled at me like we were the only two people in the world.

I smiled back, staring into nothing but oblivion.

"So that's what happens."

www.ingramcontent.com/pod-product-compliance
Lightning Source LLC
Chambersburg PA
CBHW061448210726
48287CB00007B/2407